MEDUSA

MARISSA D'ANGELO

DEDICATION

This book is dedicated to anyone who has ever felt

like they don't fit in.

Remember, no matter what…

You have a place in this world.

You are special.

ABOUT THE AUTHOR

Marissa is the author of a memoir and the Tales of Charles Island series. Marissa mostly writes fictional stories and began by journaling and writing screenplays in elementary school. She spends much of her time with her pets aside from traveling to new places and teaching. Born and raised in Connecticut, she holds New England close to her heart and many of her stories are based in the suburbs of New England.

She has a deep and profound respect for people with special needs as her first job in her field was a special educator. Marissa found her voice through writing. While in high school, she was the editor of the Arts and Entertainment section of the school newspaper. She pursued a degree in Education, minoring in English literature and Anthropology. Later, she went back to school to better understand Autism and graduated with a Master's in Special Education.

Marissa would love to hear from you. Use the links below to connect & hear about upcoming books:

2

Visit Marissa's Website:

www.mystywrites.com

Instagram:

www.instagram.com/ mysty_writes/

Amazon Page:

www.amazon.com/author/marissadangelo

PREFACE

Life wasn't always easy when you had to hide who you were…or better yet, what you were. There had not been a single day where I hadn't wondered where I came from, but focusing on adapting, despite the inevitable solidarity life would become, at times, was all I could do. Growing up, my adopted parents had always told me I was special, and although I had to hide the thing that made me who I was in order to protect those around me, they never ceased to love me.

In my early years, I had been in and out of foster homes trying to find people who would accept me as I was. To most, I was a monster. A destroyer. A killer. I was forced to flee because the very sight of my hair would turn any mortal to stone. It wasn't typical hair; each strand was a long, slithering snake waiting to cast its red piercing eyes into the soul of anyone who dared to look. And those red eyes would be the last things they would see. I had learned to wear a headwrap to conceal them, but it was nearly impossible to find parents who would adopt me given my curse.

One gloomy day when I had given up all hope and set out to run away from the foster home and raise myself, a couple came to the foster home. This time, they weren't scared of my differences because of the fact that they were mostly blind. this case, it worked out to their advantage. You see, they could be around me and not get hurt. For once, I did not have to hide who I was. And for the first time, I wouldn't fear for my loved ones' lives just because I looked at them. That was twenty years ago, and now I was living a normal woman's life: going to college, working as an intern at the local museum, and making coffees on the side. It couldn't get much more normal than that, and solidarity was long in the past, as was the curse...or so I had thought.

CHAPTER 1

GOOSEBUMPS

A domino effect. The wind billowed through, whistling as it gently caressed everything in its way. The dead of winter caused complete silence other than the sound of the relentless wind. It brushed past the chimes, filling the once silent air with a melody much reminiscent of my past, but I couldn't quite place exactly what memory it was…most of my childhood was nonexistent in my mind. Where I came from was a mystery to me, but I lay in my home pretending to be just as normal as the next person. That was what I had to do to survive. Pretend to be something, someone I was not. I felt my tangled hair moving about as I lay in bed, while the deceiving sunlight crept through the blinds.

"Another day," I sighed, reluctantly pulling myself out of bed. I walked over to the mirror and noticed just how disheveled my hair was. Days like today were the ones I was thankful I could hide behind a hair wrap.

"One day, we will find a place where I won't have to hide you," I told my snakes as I pulled them up into a bun and grabbed the silk emerald hair wrap, fitting it around my head. The longest one hissed, sticking its tongue out and gently tickling my ear before it was completely concealed. I took out the lip liner and got as close as I could to the mirror without fogging it up with my breath. As I traced the perimeter of my lips in a deep red, I grabbed the blush lipstick and guided it over my lips, smearing them together and kissing the mirror like I always did before I went out. I looked into my emerald eyes, which matched the hair wrap I had just put on, and wondered who had given me these eyes I looked at each morning? The guilt felt as if it would submerge me as quickly as a monsoon could. I snapped out of it before my mind could go further down the rabbit hole than it already had. I stepped outside my condo, feeling goosebumps rising across my skin within seconds. After rushing to my car and turning it on to warm up, I headed back inside and called my mom to check in.

"Oh, hey Meadow. How are you?" she asked.

"Cold, bitter cold," I replied through gritted teeth.

"Dad and I want you to stop by on your way home from work, okay?" she asked, ignoring my comment. Why people choose to live in a climate like this, I had no idea.

"As long as you promise not to ask how my love life is." She laughed and hung up the phone. I sighed and closed my eyes, thinking back to the memory I wish I could block out completely. The memory that made me steer clear of anyone who might have ever been interested in me. I shook my head as if that could empty my mind of it. I got up and peeked out the window. A thick sheet of ice remained over the roads. It looked like they had forgotten to salt the roads; typical Beacon Falls.

Chop Suey blasted through the speakers when I got in the car. I was definitely in a mood when I got home from work yesterday. I turned it down and looked around to find my retired neighbor shoveling snow and looking over at me with a weird expression on his face, as if I had two heads. I quickly touched my headwrap to make sure it was still there. Got it. I peeled out of my parking spot, shrugging off the interaction between my neighbor and me. It was probably all in my head…paranoia. Something I had been working on in therapy. No one knew my secret. Not even my adoptive parents. And I intended it to stay that way.

After just a few minutes, I found myself at the museum. Something was very strange. There were no cars in the parking lot; it was a ghost town. I pulled into my usual spot and checked my phone to see if there were any messages I might have missed. Not one. Was it possible I was the first one in? A gust of wind rushed past, and I felt the goosebumps spread down my arms. There was something off today. I scanned my badge and heard the buzzer as the door ahead of me unlock. A door that I wasn't sure if I even wanted to enter as my gut kept me there reluctant for a second too long and the door automatically locked again. I took a deep breath and sucked it up, scanning my badge again. The next few hours would change my life forever.

CHAPTER 2

THE PROPHECY

Everything appeared normal except at the same time, not at all. I checked my watch. 7:40. No one else had clocked in yet, but it wasn't completely unusual…I just wasn't normally as early. What wasn't normal was that things seemed to have been touched and altered slightly. One of our exhibits had artifacts within that were carefully positioned, but several of the artifacts were shifted over. Moving onward, the exhibit that seemed to have been altered the most was the Greek Mythology exhibit, which showcased several vases that hadn't been touched in ages. The museum I worked at housed many Greek and Roman artifacts, but there were also remnants of the Crusades on one entire floor. Several crusader crosses, weaponry, and armor are displayed throughout the second floor. The first floor was separated from left to right with Greek to Roman artifacts. When I took a right and walked past all the Roman god and goddess memorabilia, it seemed untouched. However, when I took a left, it wasn't until my second pass that I realized there was a book open on a table.

At first, I figured it was from the previous day, but walked toward it to see what it was and if it was even from the museum or one of our guests' belongings that had been left behind. When I edged closer, I felt my heart skip a beat. The title read, "Lady Turns People to Stone." Sweat dripped down the side of my face as I felt a rush of anxiety flush through me. I kept reading further and found a lady named Medusa, who had snakes for hair, just like me, that could turn people to stone. I felt my face grow hot, and I was thankful there was a chair beside the table because I practically melted into it. The memories I had suppressed for so long behind a wall I never dared to go past came rushing through. I could picture every moment in my mind as if it were yesterday...

"Meadow, it's time for the big dance!" Mother said.

"I can't go, sick." I coughed twice, definitely faking it.

"You know…you've never been very good at lying," she said.

"But no one really likes me. What if they pick on me?" I asked.

"Then you show them how strong you are. You smile at them and hold your head high," Mother said firmly.

"And they'll just laugh…in my face."

"Once you show people your strength and you don't back down, they will know not to pick on you again. If you stay home and cower in your bed, that will only give them more to talk about."

"Ugh!" I pulled my pillow over my face and screamed into it. "I hate when you're right."

Mother laughed and handed me the keys to the car. Neither parent ever drove because they were blind, but that worked out as an advantage to me for several reasons. They were not only safe from my curse, but I was able to drive myself places once I became of age. The only caveat was that I had to agree to drive them wherever they *wanted to go, but they were worth it. For everything they had done for me.*

I wrapped an emerald-green headwrap around my snakes—one hissing as I tucked her away last, her tongue tickling my fingers as I straightened out the wrap. "Shhh. Someday I won't have to hide you."

I heard a sound behind me, and it pulled me out of my flashback…luckily before the memory started to get bad.

"Hey!" The voice made me jump out of my seat. I quickly closed the book with my phone inside on the page and shoved it into my bag.

"Oh, Maria. I'm glad you came in! I was wondering if we were closed for the day." I wiped at the side of my face to conceal that I had been sweating. In the bitter cold, there was no excuse for this, and I was a horrible liar. Maria was a very knowledgeable scholar who came here to study from Italy. She had decided to stay once she had set down her roots at the college here. She came here to work at the museum and was an assistant professor of history. The only other thing I knew about her was that she had a love for plants and likely gardened during her free time at home. She still carried her thick Italian accent, but every word she said was fairly clear. Maria disappeared into the break room for a moment and came back without her jacket. We all had our own lockers, and she must've placed it in there. She came back out, tying up her hair in a brunette bun, leaving a few strands to hang down.

"You're never this early, Meadow. You feeling okay?" She walked up to me and gently pressed her hand against my forehead. I nearly jumped back, afraid she'd get close to—

"I'm fine." I took a step back. "Any idea what floor they're putting us on today?"

"You will stay on the Greek Mythology floor today, but I'm taking Ancient Rome!!!"

"It's almost like you make the schedule," I joked.

"Almost like." She winked at me. I walked into the break room. I felt glad to have people like her in my life sometimes. Even though she didn't know the real me— no one did for that matter—I still felt a sense of belonging in some way. But I knew I would be an outcast, just like I had been in school, if anyone ever questioned me. I put my jacket inside my locker and took out the book from my bag, sitting on the bench for a moment so I could continue reading the book. I looked around me and could see several more staff members filing in. It was close to our opening, but I needed to find out more. This woman was just like me. I opened up the book with another behind it so no one could see what I was reading, as this one belonged in the archives. I flipped through to find the page and began reading.

Prophecy.

The prophecy that has been around for ages lies in the truths of human nature. For the cursed woman with a head full of snakes has been thought to be an abomination to all of mankind. The one with the adamantine sword will strike down Medusa, beheading her and ridding the world of her monstrosity.

If words could kill.

I felt the sweat seep down the sides of my face, and my snakes became restless within the headwrap. Pushing the book into my locker, I tried not to think about what had happened. I am Meadow. I did not have to be Medusa… But how could I be just like this mythological creature that was no longer here? I had to keep reading. I skimmed with my eyes, looking for answers. Left right. Left right. Left right. …There.

The mythological creature is reborn each generation, and the cycle continues until the end of time. The two souls are drawn to one another, forevermore. The man who descends from the lineage of Zeus will be the one to behead and rid the abomination that she is from the world.

"Ladies and gentlemen, the museum is now open for public viewing. The cafeteria will open at 11 AM. Have a great day!" I closed the book like clockwork as the museum speakerphone blared out.

So, if the prophecy is right, then someone is after me and will kill me.

CHAPTER 3

PERCY

It was nearly lunchtime, and I could feel my stomach rumble. Luckily, we weren't as busy today as we had been other days, and it wasn't a weekend. I could not get my head straight for the life of me. How could I focus after reading something like that? I felt like I could barely stand on my own two legs, that they would turn to jelly at any moment, leaving me a blob on the floor, unable to walk or move. I stood beside a statue of Zeus and realized how much I wanted to escape from this section of the museum. I gave the statue a little more space and tried to hold my composure so I could just survive the rest of the shift. There was a man sitting down on the bench in front of the Athena exhibit, which held many artifacts behind a glass window. He seemed to have a notebook with him and was jotting down notes. Normally, a random man like that wouldn't have gotten my attention, but this time…there was just something off about him. He kept looking over my way. *Maybe he just has a question and isn't sure if I work here. Yeah, that's it.*

"Is there something you need more information about?" I asked, seeming to startle him. I was surprised because with how many times he had been looking over at me, surely he knew I was walking toward him. His wavy black hair reminded me of my snakes with its curls, and his brown eyes weren't just a simple brown. When he looked up at me, I could see light greens in the irises of his eyes. There was a pure innocence to him, like that of a puppy when it did something wrong and was pleading for forgiveness.

"Uhh, no, no. I am just working on a project for school," he replied, quickly closing his notebook.

"Okay, not a problem! If you need help, Liz is right over there. Otherwise, I'm going to go get some lunch." He seemed anxious, but I tried to maintain my professionalism and noticed Liz. She worked the afternoon shifts, and that meant it was lunchtime for me, and then I would spend the remainder of the afternoon organizing archives.

"Hey, wait! Could you show me where the cafeteria is?" He caught up to me when I walked away. I hesitated, knowing I had wanted to spend my lunch alone so I could read more of the book. But it could wait till the afternoon; the archives weren't going anywhere. There was also a sign right in front of us, which made me question him for a moment.

"Sure," I replied. He followed me all the way like a lost duckling, and I wondered if he had any friends. When I looked back at him, his eyes darted away from mine, and he pretended to be looking at our surroundings.

"Is the lunch any good here?" he asked, seemingly trying to make things less awkward.

"Do you want the truth or a lie?"

"I'd rather not get my hopes up, but I think that's my answer right there." He smiled. "Eh, I'll suck it up. I'm sure it's not too bad. You eat here, right?"

"Oh...you'd be surprised." I smirked and handed him a lunch tray, placing my own on the counter. I always passed by the salad, which was first on the conveyor belt. But once I got to the mashed potatoes, I just couldn't resist. I took a spoonful, then another, and plopped it down onto my plate. He looked at me with his jaw dropped, and I noticed he had a perfectly healthy salad on his tray.

"What did you say your name was?" he asked

"Meadow." I could feel my cheeks turning bright red as I felt he was judging hard. "And yours?"

"Percy. Do you want a side for your mashed potato entrée?" he joked. I rolled my eyes and laughed.

"Well, Percy, mashed potatoes are delicious, and yes, thank you. I'll have a side of bacon crumbles and shredded cheese to top them with," I replied, adding heaping spoonfuls on top as if I were attempting to make my tower of mashed potatoes as high as I possibly could.

"You're one of a kind, huh?" He laughed, plopping a much more meager amount of potatoes on his own tray. I continued on and found the steamed squash and zucchini that I so loved, then put a small piece of chicken beside everything. How ironic it was he had said that; I *am* one of a kind.

"I guess you could say that."

With that, I walked away toward the farthest table I could find, one closest to the window. Working at the museum most of the day meant that I rarely got much time to see daylight. I was always cooped up in here doing something. He sat across from me.

"Mind if I sit with you?" he asked. I nodded, wishing I could just have lunch alone, but for some strange reason, I felt a pull toward him. I dove into my potatoes so I could keep my mouth busy before I said something stupid.

"What made you want to work at this museum?" he asked. I finished chewing my mashed potatoes and swallowed, staring hard out the window, deciding exactly how I wanted to answer this question. No one had ever asked me, and my parents had always just assumed it was because I liked history.

"For my entire life, I had always wondered where I came from. I was in and out of foster homes at an early age and always enjoyed learning about history. I feel that knowing history is knowing one's self, and the history of our world is like a puzzle made of little pieces that can be placed together to form the bigger picture," I said.

"Wow, I didn't expect all that. So, you've always wondered about your history, and that has made you interested in the history of our world in general? That's pretty neat," Percy answered.

"And what brings you to this museum?" I asked.

"I like history too." The pause he gave before he finally answered made me feel like he wanted to say something else entirely. I accepted his answer, but I knew there was more to him, and I was going to find out.

CHAPTER 4

BREAKING NEWS

"With the breaking news of the recent thefts at other museums, this museum is now closed until further investigation is completed. Please take your belongings and proceed to the nearest exit. The museum will offer you a full refund for today's visit. We apologize for any and all inconveniences this may cause. Thank you and have a nice day," the speaker announced.

Percy and I both looked up at one another, full of confusion. I thought back to this morning and the book that had been laid open on the table. *Was it possible that something had been stolen from one of the exhibits and I had completely missed it? But more importantly, was there someone out there searching for me?*

I felt my cheeks grow red. The secret I hid for as long as I could remember might be out, and there wasn't anything I could do about it. My mind went back to the flashback from so long ago.

Voices of the crowds within bellowed out before I could even make it into the school gym. I just needed to make it through one hour, and that would be it. Balloons framed the entrance, and kids were still being dropped off. One by one, with their friends. Me? I did not have any. Despite my efforts to keep my secret hidden, I was still somehow ostracized. As soon as I walked into the gym, it appeared to be a winter wonderland. The walls were no longer the mustard yellow I remembered from gym class, but instead lined with snowflake wallpaper. At the center of the ceiling was a disco ball that illuminated the dance floor.

"Meadow!! I had no idea you were coming!" another outcast from my math class was always much more optimistic than I. Everyone else already had their cliques and it seemed that she had been alone at the dance. I could tell she felt lucky to see me and finally not be alone. It was no surprise she was here, but I knew she probably felt lucky to see me being that everyone else already had their cliques.

"Hey Sarah, definitely not here by choice." I laughed. Her powdery-pink dress puffed out at the sides; she reminded me of one of my old Barbie dolls that I always hated, but kept because it had been a gift. Her dirty-blonde hair was up in a bun with a few strands hanging down by the sides of her rosy face.

"Well…let's make the most of it!" she screamed, grabbing my arm and pulling me through groups of people until we made our way to the middle of the dance floor. The DJ blared out "Wannabe" by the Spice Girls, and Sarah just about lost her mind if she hadn't already. She took both of my hands in hers and jumped up and down like she was a kid at a sleepover jumping on the bed.

"You're crazy!!" I yelled over the music, but couldn't help but smile because this was the most fun I had in my entire life. It was the most accepted I had felt.

"And you're not?!" she screamed back.

We jumped around like that for the next few songs until we both tired out completely and a slow song came on. That was our cue to head over to the food… toward something that would change the entire night.

"Meadow, it's time to go. They're kicking us out," Percy snapped, pulling me out of it. At first, his lips had just been moving. I couldn't seem to hear anything coming out of them, but then it clicked.

"You're forgetting I work here," I answered, glad the flashback had been interrupted.

"I'm sure they don't want you here either, though, if they're closing!" he said.

"Well, I've got to go grab my things from the staff room, but it was really nice to meet you!" I said, rushing away with my lunch. I tossed the remnants of my loaded mashed potatoes into the trash and placed the tray above it. When I looked back, Percy was gone, and the table was completely empty. I was surprised because he wasn't even finished eating when I had left. I turned back around and continued on toward my locker. Just because the museum was closing to visitors didn't mean that the staff had to clear out as well. I had waited several hours to finally open that book back up and read more about Medusa and the prophecy.

"You're not gone yet?" Maria asked as she got her jacket back on. I was hoping to come in here alone so no one would see me leave with the book, but a little longer wouldn't hurt.

"Nahh, I got a little distracted." A warm sensation stretched over my cheeks, and I could tell I was turning red.

"Oh...say no more. We all saw you head to lunch with that boy," she laughed.

"Good, I wasn't planning to say any more."

"Ooph, hostile, Meadow."

"Okay, he's kinda cute," I admitted. "But I'll never see him again, so don't worry."

"He'll be back," she reassured me. "Anyway, can you believe they're closing early?! The other museums have missing artifacts from several exhibits. No one knows why."

"Well, I'm sure they are going to sell them for money." I thought back to the open book that was beside the Athenian exhibit in the Greek Mythology section. Could it be that they stole something from there too?

"All the cash registers had a full till. It was the one exhibit that was targeted. I'm glad we're closing. Who knows if the thief would've come in and hurt one of us. Luckily, they seem to come after hours?"

"Do you know if anything missing from any of our exhibits?" I asked.

"Not that I know of. Why? Do you think the thief has already struck our museum?" Her eyebrows were furrowed, and she seemed to be riddled with even more questions. I thought about telling her about the book, but this seemed dangerous to get involved in. I remembered Sarah from years ago and how Maria reminded me of her. I couldn't let Maria get too close, or she would get hurt too.

"No, probably not. You're right; it's best they're letting us leave. Whoever this is that's taking artifacts seems dangerous. Who knows what they're capable of."

"Yeah, to steal winged sandals from Hermes, and the so-called Helm of invisibility…it's just a tad strange if you ask me." She put on her jacket and gloves and looked over at me with sympathy. "Just keep thinking about dream boy, and don't let this worry you. He will be back for you. I just know it."

Maria finally left, and I was alone in the staff room. I took a deep breath and opened up my locker, grabbing my bag and jacket when I jumped in my place.

"All staff and employees, please exit as the museum is going into lockdown mode to keep the artifacts safe. Again, all staff and employees please exit as soon as possible." And with that, I grabbed my backpack and headed out to my car. Whatever was going on, I felt like it had something to do with me for some reason. I must've been one of the last ones out of there. There wasn't a single car in the parking lot besides mine and one other, which I assumed belonged to another staff member. My phone started ringing, and I knew it could only be one person who must've been listening to the news and worried about me...per the usual.

"Mom, I'm okay," I said before she could speak.

"Oh, good honey. Come here after work. We heard all the museums are closing for further investigation. Was yours hit too?" she asked, and I wondered why she wanted to know when she likely already knew the answer.

"Not that I know of." I left the small tidbit out about this morning when an exhibit had definitely been tampered with. There was no sense in making her even more worried about something that might be totally unrelated. Staff at the museum moved things around in the exhibit sometimes to study them or take inventory.

"Okay, I'll see you soon? We're making chicken cutlets for dinner. Love you!" She hung up without even waiting for a response from me, which she absolutely loved to do. It confirmed my answer had to be yes and I had no choice but to come now. All day I had waited for a chance to look through the book, and hopefully in the privacy of my family's home, I finally could.

CHAPTER 5

FLASHBACK

The chase. It seemed life always involved a never-ending chase. Perhaps the outcome or goal differed for each person, but no matter what, everyone chased after something. All my life, I saw people chasing similar things like money, love, or tangible items. But for me, it was different. I yearned to find who I was. And I'm sure other people are on a similar adventure, but most of my life I felt like I was an outcast and like I had been sent here from another world. Each day, I hoped and dreamed I would wake up in the morning and find that I could finally be myself. I could walk into a crowded room as myself and no one would get hurt. No one would die. You see, it was that night that had changed me forever. It was that night that I had wished I had never been born or, at the very least, locked up for everyone else's sake.

I looked at my parents' house and stalled going in because I couldn't get my mind off the book and Percy. Whenever the museum opened back up, I had a feeling he would come back. He seemed like a nice guy, but you can't always judge a book by its cover.

The silhouette of Mom's shadow beamed through the curtains. If I knew her, she already had everything made and was keeping it warm in the oven. While she was partially blind, it was incredible how much she could still do considering. Dad enjoyed listening to music in his music room upstairs. I thought of him as the Ray Charles of my life since he was able to play several instruments. They were always the perfect pair; they had been made for one another. Sometimes, it made me feel that much more alone since I doubted anyone in this universe was anywhere remotely close to my soulmate. I unzipped my bag that was lying on the seat so I could get the book out and quickly skim through some of its pages before heading in. It felt remarkably light earlier, and as soon as I got the zipper down all the way, I realized the book was…gone. Impossible. I had it in my locker the entire day! I shoved my hand in each compartment despite knowing the book wouldn't be in there because it was way too small. Where could it have gone?!

A knock came on the window of my door. Mom. I turned the key and took it out of the ignition and opened the door, hugging her.

"You've been out here an awfully long time. Everything okay?" she asked. The hug was what I needed right then. Her short hair tickled my cheek, and I could feel the tear that had streamed down my cheek freeze in the frigid air. My teeth started to chatter, and more tears came. I thought back to that night…that sad, sad night that had started off so well, but ended so horribly.

That was so much fun, I didn't think I would say this, but I'm so glad that I came." I could barely catch my breath from dancing so much. Sarah's face glistened with sweat and glitter as she was downing a bottle of water. I did the same.

"I told you!! You don't have to know many people to make it fun. As long as you have at least one person, you're in good company. Hey look over there. They've got a whole baked potato station! That's kinda random, isn't it?" she asked. I chuckled and headed over. That was the start of my love of loaded baked potatoes. They had all the works: bacon bits, butter, sour cream, chives, shredded cheese of many different kinds. I walked over and waited for Sarah to fill her plate before grabbing my own when that wretched song came on...the song that would always remind me of that night for the rest of my life. The soft piano came in as the dance floor cleared and people looked for their significant others to dance with. They put their arms around one another's waists and slowly moved left to right. Some looked into each other's eyes while others rested their heads on the other's shoulder.

"I'm going under, and this time I feel there's no one to save me," was the first line. The first line that was embedded into my mind so much that I had it tattooed across my forearm. Sometimes in life, you didn't have to be in water to feel like you were drowning. To feel like you *couldn't breathe. Sometimes, you could breathe perfectly fine but, at the same time, feel as though you were gasping for air. Gasping for a chance in this world. Someone to save you. Even if it was from yourself.*

Sarah had gone off with a boy she always talked to in homeroom while I stayed there with my empty plate. One of the most popular boys, Jeffrey, on the school wrestling came over and smiled at me. He held out his hand, and I wondered why he would ask me of all people to dance with him when we didn't even talk much. But the night was going so well that I thought of this as the cherry on top.

"Meadow, will you dance with me?" he asked. His friends snickered and laughed nearby, but I didn't think much of it. I placed my shaky hand in his as it enveloped mine, and he brought me to the dance floor. We danced for maybe a whole thirty seconds when I saw Sarah wink from just a few feet away, cheering me on as any good friend would. And that was the last I saw of her alive.

Everything that happened next was a blur. There was laughter and then silence. It all happened so fast. I felt my headwrap fall as someone yanked it from behind me, and while I had just been looking at Sarah, her eyes began to roll into the back of her head. Her hair crumpled and turned to ash that fell to the floor. I felt my snakes hissing around me—scared, exposed, and betrayed. Sarah's pink cheeks paled and turned to stone. It spread like a rapid disease without a cure to her entire face and then her body. Bit by bit, she was frozen in time like everyone else in the room. I felt Jeffrey grow cold and stiff in my arms. I had to yank myself away, and that's when I noticed Jeffrey's friends from the varsity team standing in a group. They must've been behind Jeffrey all along and planned this as some prank. No one had known about the snakes though. If they had known, they wouldn't have dared to take off the headwrap that kept them safe. My snakes managed to strike from every angle as I realized I was now in a room surrounded by stone statues. I felt my legs turn to jelly, and I fell forward onto the floor, smashing my fists down in agony. I kept going and going until my knuckles bled from the impact. The song was still playing as the DJ had also turned to stone. Somehow, it felt as though an earthquake had come and the entire building shook, causing the stone statues of my classmates to shatter to the ground. The last line of the song solemnly *blared out, and I made myself a promise to never let my guard down again for as long as I lived, to never get close to someone again. For as long as I held this curse, I could never keep my loved ones safe.*

"I let my guard down and then you pulled the rug…I was getting kinda used to being someone you loved."

"Mom, I missed you." I felt the tears stream down my cheeks. There was not much more that I could say. The missing book, the random guy, the thefts… everything. The instability that my life had become caused the pain of the past to come rushing in like a waterfall. And I had no protection.

CHANCE

"So tell us more about this guy." Mom gushed about Percy even though I had just told her that I had to show him the cafeteria at the museum.

"It's someone I will likely never see again, so don't get too excited." I rolled my eyes, scooping more mashed potatoes onto my plate.

"If he likes you, he'll come back. That's just how the world works," Dad chimed in. Part of me hoped I would see him again, but remembering my flashback…I hoped he wouldn't for his own sake.

"Not if he knows what's good for him!" I said with my mouth full.

"You sell yourself short, sweetie. Anyone would be lucky to have you," Mom said.

"Well, there's a bigger problem at hand. I'm unsure when the museum will open back up, and there's been a series of thefts at the sister museums. It's weird because they could be stealing cash and other items, but instead, they're stealing specific artifacts from Greek exhibits." I thought back to the book that went missing from my backpack. The thief may have been in the museum the same day that I had...who else would think to steal something out of my backpack like that? And from the staff room? The only person I remember seeing consistently was Maria. But it couldn't have been her, could it?

"There's a lot of money in that industry. They could be selling the artifacts to third-party dealers to make money off of them," Dad said. He was always so knowledgeable about this stuff.

"I hope they will be open for the big showcase in just a few days. Without those artifacts and with heavy surveillance, the event may be canceled."

"I bet they'll still have it," Mom reassured me. "So back to Percy..."

"Guys!!" I yelped, growing red in the face. Dad walked over to his piano and began playing Beethoven's 5th symphony as if we were all on some kind of show and this was the background music.

"Duh-duh-duh-DUNNNN." He chuckled as he played.

"I'm surprised I haven't ended up in the funny farm yet with you two," I joked.

"There's still time!" Mom called over from the sink as she washed them and laughed. I walked over to the piano and started messing with Dad's song, playing "Ode to Joy" to contrast with his solemn tune choice. From an early age, Dad taught me how to play the piano and signed me up for lessons. It was very rare that I played, but the chords to certain songs stuck in my mind. The new remix that we came up with was actually pretty catchy, and I wondered if anyone had ever merged the two songs before. We played for a while longer and Dad turned to me, arms out to give me a hug. I wrapped my arms around him and felt safer in that moment. Although I still had to hide one of the biggest things that made me who I was from them, there were moments that they made me feel normal; as if I was just a normal girl all along, raised by a normal family and working my normal job. But what was normal anyway?

"Give him a chance, Med." His words were earnest and genuine. Coming from my dad, who never thought any guy was good enough to be with me, this meant a lot.

"Okay, but if this blows up in my face, I'll be coming for you," I half-joked. We talked a little more before I told them I had to go. When I got to my car, a silly idea came into my mind. I wanted to go back to the museum to see if the book had possibly fallen out in my locker. I texted Maria.

Me: Any news on whether or not the museum will be open tomorrow?

She almost immediately replied.

Maria: Of course we're going in! Heightened security, though. Be ready to feel like you are in a castle armed to the teeth.

Me: It's better than the alternative! See you tomorrow!

I pushed my phone back into my bag and left, heading to the museum. I had a key after all. I'd just pop in, get the book and head right back out. It's got to be in my locker. Got to be...

DÉJÀ VU

I almost felt as though I was getting déjà vu because of the lack of people in the parking lot as there were earlier this morning, but this time it actually made sense. The museum was closed to the public since it was nighttime, but I couldn't help but feel an edge in the air from the early closure. Was I allowed to be here as a staff member? Would I be one of the people accused if caught? Surely there were cameras everywhere that would show me going in, getting something from my locker, and then leaving. Plain and simple as that. I checked the clock and realized I had been sitting in my car debating whether or not to go in for the past twenty minutes. My car lights had already turned off since I had been sitting for so long. That's when I saw a hooded figure walking toward the back of the museum, where the staff usually walked in. He was tall, thin and looked to be in a hurry. The place had been deserted before he walked by. I took out my phone and considered calling the authorities, but something in me made me put it away. I felt compelled to check it out myself because, for some reason, the thefts felt like a personal attack in a way. I never believed in coincidences and the fact that the book lay open to the prophecy of Medusa and the items that were stolen were items that Perseus had used in the myth…it was just too "coincidental" that this thief was targeting those things alone from museums.

He appeared to swipe a badge and go right in without a problem. There was no one I could think of who would've come here at night. Everyone had families to tend to, and well, Maria was likely busy with her nose in a book. I put my bag over my shoulder and headed over to the door he had just gone through. The cool air made my teeth chatter and my hands shake as I rummaged through my bag for my badge. I went through every single zipper, and there was nothing. I pulled out all my stuff from my bag and tried to feel around for anything, but it was completely empty. There was nothing inside it. When I stood up and put my bag over my shoulder, the hooded figure was on the other side of the door about to make his or her exit. I still couldn't see their face because they were wearing a mask, but they looked like a deer in headlights, scared of me when it should have been the other way around.

The hooded figure continued to make their way out and handed me my badge. I caught a glimpse of his dark eyes before he ran off into the woods, leaving no trace except for me and the badge that he had somehow taken. I could hear alarms going off from inside the museum. We didn't have many sensors within, but they must have installed them when we closed earlier. His touch sent a shock through my body and made me feel like I had just been slightly electrocuted. As the alarms sang out, police cars rolled in, one by one, forming a circle around the perimeter of the museum, closing me in so that even if I wanted to, I could not leave.

"Put your hands up! an older cop said as he held out his gun, ready to shoot. I glanced toward the forest, wishing the cops had arrived just a few minutes earlier, but followed his order.

"Thank you for cooperating. This is a crime scene –""Meadow?!" I heard Liz's voice.

"Let her go. She's one of our employees," she pleaded. I looked over at her, thankful, but felt myself continuing to be handcuffed and restrained. I could feel my snakes grow restless. I whispered to them to calm down, silently enough for no one to hear.

"The museum is closed, so why is one of your employees here?" one of the other cops asked. Liz looked over to me for that answer, and the cops' gazes followed.

"I left something in my locker," I admitted. It was true.

"And you come at a time after we've just locked down?!" she asked, clearly forgetting the cops were around us for a split second.

"I know, I just thought I'd grab it from the locker and then leave real quick. Now I realize I shouldn't have come," I admitted. I could feel the handcuffs loosen, and that's when I debated whether or not to tell them about the hooded figure. I pursed my lips and decided on the latter.

"Let her go. But if there are any questions, we'll know who to ask," ordered a man I assumed was the chief. I gulped down, knowing as soon as the museum opened up tomorrow and they realized things were missing—because they likely were taken from that man I saw—I'd be interrogated first. I guess that would be a tomorrow problem. His dark eyes haunted me as I felt he stared deep into my soul.

"Okay everyone, false alarm. Let's all go home and get a good night's rest. Who knows what tomorrow'll bring," the man who I had presumed was the chief said, and everyone walked back to their cars. My heart was still racing, and I felt I could run several miles with how much adrenaline was rushing through me. Liz stayed behind after all the police left and looked me directly in the eyes.

"Meadow, I understand what you did was harmless, but I think you are underestimating how dangerous this man is," she said. "There is more to the story than you know. The news and media have not released all the facts."

"What happened?" was the obvious next question.

"There have been staff members reported missing and dead…" she confirmed. I felt like my heart skipped a beat, and I could hear a hiss coming from underneath my headwrap. But why did he let me go? There was nothing more I could say to Liz. My lips couldn't find any words. I wanted so badly to confide in her, but now this mess seemed even worse than what it started as. Liz must have been able to tell how tense I was as she pulled me in for a hug and let me continue on my way. I drove home in silence—not wanting to involve anyone else in this. And after I repeatedly checked the locks to my apartment and looked in the closets and bathtub to see if he had somehow followed me home or been waiting for me, I stared up at my bedroom ceiling, thinking of those dark eyes.

KILLER

The buzzer went off, and I heard the sirens ringing in my ears like they had the previous night. A relentless, throbbing pain in my head just wouldn't go away. I took some Tylenol to help ease my headache, but it was no use. The snakes on my head felt dull and without life, like they too, were just getting by. A quick English muffin with butter was all I had time for as I had to be at work by 7 a.m. and it was already 6:30. I briefly glanced at my phone to find two unread messages, one from Maria and the other from a number I hadn't yet saved to my contacts.

Maria: We will be coming in today, heightened security.

Me: See you soon

I presumed Maria had no idea what had happened last night and didn't know if it was even worth giving her the details, not this early anyway. When we opened up today, there was no knowing what the thief would've taken, if anything at all. I brushed my teeth and quickly tied my snakes back, whispering to them gently, "Sorry guys. Someday, I won't have to hide you…I hope."

The chill of the outside air woke me right up like a jolt went through my entire body. But something felt off. I got in my car as I normally would any day and headed into work. It felt like it took forever to get there, but when I finally pulled in, cop cars swarmed the parking lot just as they had the previous night. I thought about the text that Maria had sent me and the "heightened security." Is this what she meant by that? Who would bother coming to a museum that looked like a legitimate crime scene? I slowly got out of my car and saw Maria sobbing by the front entrance. Something had happened between the time Maria sent me the text and now. With the way she was sobbing, there was no way she could have held her phone steady enough to send out a message. I got out of my car and rushed to her side. At first, some cops went to hold me back, but when I showed them my badge—the badge I just got back from the thief—they allowed me through toward the entrance. Maria looked down at her feet at first, then looked up at me, and all I saw was horror in her eyes.

"She…she…she's dead," she stuttered.

"Who?"

"Liz." She nearly stumbled over and fell to the ground, but I caught her and she began sobbing again into my shoulder.

"What? No…this has gotta be some kind of mistake. I just saw her last night!" I exclaimed and shifted Maria over to a nearby. I needed to talk to the chief. He gestured for me to come inside his cop car.

"Normally, we would not bring you into an active crime scene, but here…so you can see for your own eyes." He clasped his hand over his mouth and nose as if to block out the stench. When I went in, I could feel my snakes tense, which they only did when there was a problem and they had to be on alert. I rubbed my headwrap in an attempt to quiet them. Right when I walked in, I couldn't help but cover my mouth and nose as well. I wished I could cover my eyes too. Maria was right. Liz was dead. She had been murdered. She still had her hat on from when I saw her outside, and her hair had been carefully tucked away into it. I remembered her long, blonde hair. It appeared as though the murderer had taken one of the adamantine swords and pierced it through her chest. But that wasn't the worst part.

"What is this?" I asked, peering slightly closer to Liz's body. A book lay open in her hands, and her eyes were taped open, staring at it. As soon as I was able to get just a little bit closer, the chief pulled me back, but it was just after I caught a glimpse of what page the book was open to. It was the book I had been retrieving from my locker, and it was open to the prophecy…just as I had found it the previous morning. Liz had a giant red X spray-painted on her chest as if someone was trying to cross her off some list.

The chief led me outside, and I walked over to Maria, who was now sitting on a bench with her head in her hands. I slumped down beside her, and that's when the guilt sank in. It all started when I got into work yesterday morning. When I saw that book, I should've turned it in as evidence, especially after finding out about the recent thefts. But then…and even then, I hadn't told anyone about my exchange with the thief and how he had my badge. If I had told Liz last night, she would've been more cautious or told the authorities to check out the inside of the museum. After the cops and I left, Liz was the only one there, and she must have gone inside. But what did she go in for? Had she left something in there, too? It didn't make much sense. She had just given me a warning about going in there alone after the string of thefts, but she did the opposite of the advice she had given me. The red X…the prophecy…adamantine sword…if I knew anything about Greek mythology, it was the story of Medusa. I always sympathized with her since she was born that way and couldn't help it. I never told anyone, but oddly, I could relate to her because of my snakes. While young children watched fairy tales and heard stories of princesses and princes, imagining themselves, I always related to a mythological creature that never had a happy ending. It was very true to life because there seemed to be no happy ending in store for me.

"Maria," I weakly said. She looked over at me and reminded me of a child who was lost and looking for her mother. I thought about how scary it must have been for her to move all this way from Italy and not know a single soul.

"If I had come in a few minutes earlier, maybe I could have helped her," Maria said. I felt that. I certainly felt that to the core.

"You are not responsible; the sicko who did this is," I said as I heard one of my snakes hiss.

"What was that?" she asked, looking up and around at where the sound could have come from.

"I don't know, I heard it too," I said, trying to look as confused as possible.

"What should we do?" Maria asked. I was thankful she changed the subject and didn't start asking about my headwrap.

"I guess we've gotta go home..."

"Oh no you don't. Remember last night? We told you there'd be some questions, and we're going to be asking you a few things, so you make yourself comfortable right here," the chief said as he walked by, seeming to have eavesdropped on our conversation.

"Last night?" Maria cocked her head to the side.

"Ugh, I came here to grab something from my locker, and I ran into Liz. She told me that it wasn't safe here and to leave."

"But how would the cops know that?"

"Well, an alarm was set off inside, and it automatically made a call to the police. You were right when you said they had heightened security."

"And you didn't think to tell me?!" She stood up and crossed her arms over her chest.

"Well, I didn't want to worry you and didn't think much of it, but now I see."

"So, you may have been the last one to see Liz alive then? No wonder they have questions for you. Why did she come back here anyway?"

"Me. I guess I set off an alarm, and she was coming here to meet me along with the police. She told them to let me go, that I worked here. She wouldn't have been here alone if it weren't for me." As if my heart couldn't sink any deeper in my chest, it did.

"Alright, you. We'll make this quick. Come with us," the chief said, guiding me over toward his car.

THE LIST

"I'm not going to bring you down to the department," he called back from the driver's side of his car. I couldn't get comfortable in the backseat and couldn't help but squirm around.

"Am I under arrest?"

"No, but we need to be very careful in this investigation because it seems the suspect may have been inserting himself into our investigations. He could even be one of my own, someone I would least expect. I don't have any questions for you, but I do need to give you some information…for your own safety," he said.

"Okay," was all I could say.

"I know you must be in shock from losing your boss. I don't know how close you two were, but I feel like you need to know this killer is methodical in his ways. We hadn't released it to the public due to the ongoing investigation, but there were also people found murdered at the last two museums where thefts occurred."

"And what does this have to do with me?"

"Well—"

"Shouldn't Maria be here too?" I asked.

"That's what I want to talk to you about. We found a list of names, and the first two were people that had already been murdered while the third was Liz's..." He paused, looking back at me.

"And? What's the fourth name?"

"Yours."

I felt my snakes grow restless. I had to rub my head in circles to calm them, but I felt the opposite of calm myself.

"What do I do??" I asked.

"Live your life as you normally would, and we will have an agent follow your lead so we can find him before anything happens," he replied. And in this instance, I felt thankful for my snakes. As much of a curse as they were, they offered me the protection I needed. There seemed to be nothing the cops could do. Whoever the hooded figure was, he spared me for some reason right before he murdered Liz. But why me? And why Liz?

"Why not Maria? I mean, I'm glad she didn't make the list, but I don't understand what the correlation is between these people."

"We think this man is in some kind of hallucinogenic state where he thinks the Greek myths are real. He is after anyone who somewhat resembles the Medusa creature. He might as well have escaped the psych ward," he said.

I half-hoped that I could just turn myself in and allow him to find me so no one else had to die. I realized that Liz's hair always being back likely made him think she had something to hide and, well... my headwrap. I got out of the car and walked over to the bench where Maria was sitting, and she looked a little calmer now. I wondered whether I should share all the details of what I had just found out. But I couldn't. I couldn't bring myself to say it, or it would feel that much more real.

"You all right?" Maria asked.

"Yeah, just feeling guilty is all. I wish I could've done something to help. I feel so bad for Liz. I don't know if I will ever be able to work here again. I won't be able to *not* think about what happened. I wish I could block out the scene of the crime, but it's forever embedded in my head now."

"Like a nightmare, only you can't wake up," Maria said, nodding her head. "If you need anything, I'm a text away. I'm going to head home and try to process what just happened…if that's even possible."

"Same goes for you, Maria. I'll keep my ringer on," I said, flipping the switch on the side of my phone. She walked away and quickly got in her car, pulling out within seconds. She must've been waiting for me to finish talking to the chief of police. I stayed there on the bench, staring toward the woods where the hooded figure had wandered off to last night. Out of the corner of my eye, I saw Percy walk toward the entrance looking confused. I heard the police tell him that the museum was closed for further investigation. He looked over my way and we locked eyes. In a way, my heart felt a little fuller because the last time I saw him was when things were somewhat normal. But now, everything was a mess. His wavy black hair was smoothed to the side, and his eyes looked lighter than usual today. He looked softly at me and sat beside me on the bench where Maria had just sat.

"What's going on?" he asked. "Are you okay?"

"Well, I'm okay…" Okay was an understatement.

"What happened?"

"It's too much to say," I admitted. It really was. Where would I begin? Oh, I have snakes for hair, and I can turn people to stone. And with this curse, there is now a person who is trying to find me and kill me. He has been tracking down anyone who is remotely similar to me in any way. Oh yeah, and there's this prophecy where a man named Perseus must kill me according to the fate of the world. And in each generation, there are people like him and people like me. There is not a single story where I do not end up dead. So yeah, that sums it up!

"I've got time," was all he said. I kept quiet, and he gently took my hands in his own, staring into my eyes. "For some reason, I am drawn to you, and there's nothing you can say that will scare me away, so don't worry."

"Is that a challenge?" I asked, knowing full well that there was something.

"If you want it to be."

"Percy, she's dead. My boss. Liz is dead." The words seemed to seal her fate even more and made what happened that much more real.

"What happened?" he asked. "Well, never mind. Let me take you away from here, okay? If you don't want to talk about it, you don't have to." At that moment, I appreciated him so much and wished he had come into my life sooner. If I had someone like him, life wouldn't be all that lonely. He stood up and put out his hand for me to take. When he looked down at me, I hesitated to take his hand. I didn't want him to get hurt too. It seemed that anyone who was close to me was taken from me. I thought about Mom and Dad. I worried for them too.

"I don't know…"

"What if I promised some delicious potatoes?" he asked. I couldn't help but smile. And I felt a pit of guilt in my gut for finding some joy in a time like this. But I looked back at the cordoned-off entrance to the museum that had once been a refuge—a sanctuary for me to seek comfort. I looked back at his hand, then locked eyes with him and took his hand.

THE RISK

There are times when most seek comfort in sticking to the same decisions, routines and the same old lifestyle choices that they have always made. But when you continue to do the same thing, the outcomes are usually similar as well.

I told him I would drive because it didn't feel right to let someone I barely knew drive me to who knows where. I knew better than that, or so I thought. He directed me with left and right turns until we reached a clearing. I pulled onto a dirt path and turned off the car, crossing my arms and looking over at him. I could tell he sensed my hesitation as he too hesitated and his eyebrows lifted in a sincere look.

"The strange man brings the stupid girl to a deserted place only to…" I began, but he cut me off.

"Only to bring her to a really beautiful place that frosted over from the cold," he finished my sentence with a completely different ending than what I had originally intended.

"I was thinking something more on the darker side." I admitted. He smirked and walked around the car, putting his hand out for me to take. I hesitated for a moment, then placed my hand in his, taking the risk. I let go of his hand as soon as I got out of the car and locked it, looking back, wishing I was still there or, better yet, had just gone home, but I looked at the way he stared back at me so gently and it was hard to resist. The way he barely clasped his hand around mine, as if he was afraid that he'd break me. But little did he know, I was the one afraid of getting too close to him.

The overnight dusting of snow glistened, giving the tree branches an ethereal glow as the sun shimmered all over. It was a blanket of deception in that all you saw looked beautiful, but the cold could shake you to your very core.

"Do you need my jacket?" he asked, clearly noticing as I trembled and my teeth chattered.

"No, no. I'm fine," I lied. The last thing I wanted was to take his jacket and act as if we were a thing. I wasn't letting him in more than I already had.

"That's believable." He turned back to me and winked, then continued on farther. I wondered how much longer I was going to follow him.

"So…are you bringing me out here to never be seen again? My parents are expecting me for dinner." I made up a believable. He stopped in his tracks and didn't answer. I caught up to him, but he wasn't looking over at me; instead, he was staring straight ahead. I looked out and saw nothing out of the ordinary. When he still didn't answer, I walked in front of him, blocking his view. He didn't even blink. I waved my hand in front of his eyes.

"Hello?? Anybody home??" I asked, remembering my grandfather Louis and how he would always say that when someone wasn't answering him. It was funny because sometimes, he would knock on their head as if it were a door and he was seeing if there was anything inside.

He looked at me with shock in his eyes and placed one finger over my lips, silencing me before I could say another word. With his other hand, he slowly pushed my shoulder so I faced the same direction he did. When he turned me away from him, I looked out and felt my heart skip a beat. As the last snow came, animals were beginning to come out of hibernation, and with that...about twenty feet ahead of us was a black bear. I hadn't seen it at first but could hear it snort as it looked for food. I wished I hadn't said anything because it was staring straight at us now and we were right in a clearing, completely exposed and vulnerable. I knew what I had to do.

"Close your eyes," I said, without looking back at Percy.

"What? Why?" he said. "We need to make loud sounds to scare it away."

"Please trust me." I glanced back for a moment to see his questioning eyes, but I was desperate. "Percy, close your eyes!" I screamed, hearing the snarls of the bear as it edged closer. When I turned back around, the bear was charging at us, and I ripped off my headwrap as fast as I could, unleashing my snakes completely. My head hit the ground like a ton of bricks smacked me out of nowhere. A piercing pain came into my chest as the blood seeped out. I stared back up at the bear, but it was no longer a threat. Before me, the bear had become stone and frozen in place like a statue. Right when I pulled the headwrap off, it had pushed me down and pressed its sharp claws into my chest. I quickly wrapped my head again, concealing my snakes.

"Percy?" I whispered, groaning in pain, not knowing if he too had been turned to stone.

"Is it safe to look?" he asked. I felt a tear stream down my cheek as I lay there.

"If you're not squeamish at the sight of blood," I answered.

"Meadow!" He kneeled by my side, looking over at the bear, then back at me. I knew there were likely hundreds of questions swarming his mind, but he seemed to be the most worried about me.

"Is it that bad?" I asked, trying to raise my head in a failed attempt.

"Meadow, what happened?" he began and lifted his backpack off his arms, pulling out an emergency kit. "Okay, don't worry about explaining, just lie very still."

"I don't think I have another choice if I want to," I joked, feeling weak and dizzy from the blood loss. He pulled out supplies and tore off his shirt, wrapping it around my chest, slowly pulling it under my back so he could wrap it more tightly. He pulled out a Powerade and placed a straw inside, gently lifting my head with his hand and pushing the straw into my mouth. I raised an eyebrow in confusion as to why he had all these supplies to begin with. But I wasn't in a place to ask. I drank the Powerade and felt some energy come back to me.

"We have to bring you to the hospital," he said.

"NO!" I screamed. "I mean...no." I lowered my tone, realizing how loud I was.

"You lost a lot of blood. You probably need a transfusion."

"I'll be okay. I just need some rest." I closed my eyes and felt like I could have fallen asleep right there and then.

"Oh no you don't."

"Just a little nap," I said, sleepily. I could see him, then he faded away like clouds hazed over his body. I felt those clouds lift my body, or was he carrying me? A daze settled over me, lulling me into unconsciousness.

CHAPTER 11

THE SECRET

No matter how much you tried to hide something, it would always come out in some way, shape, or form. I tried to keep who I was a secret, not just for my sake, but for everyone else's. My true form was not just something that would be studied like a guinea pig in some lab for the rest of my days, but it was also dangerous to know who I was. I opened my eyes, staring straight up at a ceiling that looked very different from mine at my home. It was pitch black, and a swarm of stars laid out over it. It almost felt like I was outside if it weren't for the four walls around me.

I went to raise my head, instantly feeling the pain in my chest. The pain came, and memories of the bear flooded back. I lifted my hand to my chest and felt a wrapping over it. I shivered and pulled the blanket up farther to cover me more. The last I remembered was being with Percy walking and then we saw a bear...oh, and I pulled off my headwrap to protect us against the bear. I heard someone snore near me and slowly propped up my head so I could see.

Percy was by the window in a chair, fast asleep. He must have brought me back to his place after the bear attack. But what was even more surprising was the fact that he listened to me when I told him to close his eyes. A bear had been coming to attack, and he followed my lead. I didn't know anyone else who would've trusted in me that much in such a crucial split second. I still felt like we didn't know each other enough, but for some reason, I also felt like I had known him my entire life. It was a weird feeling, like we had met in another lifetime and we were just carrying on what we hadn't finished before.

I carefully lifted my head to look at him again as he breathed deeply in and out. His dark hair looked a mess, but it made him that much sexier. A little facial hair lined the bottom half of his face, and his lips came together in a soft crease. I closed my eyes, feeling safe for once in a very long time. But then I thought about the cordoned-off crime scene and Liz…Liz, who was guilty by association and never should have been targeted in the first place. She was collateral damage along with everyone else who had lost their lives. The guilt sank in deep and hurt even more than the wound from the bear that tried to claw its way through me. I felt a tear stream down my cheek and thought back to the dance with Sarah. I put my head in my hands and let the tears stream out to the point I was hyperventilating and in full panic mode. The wall I had so carefully put up to suppress all the bad was crumbling down and flooding out, and I couldn't contain it any longer. I felt arms drape around me and pull me in. I didn't have to look up to know it was Percy. He said nothing, but slowly rubbed my back in circles. Sometimes, there was nothing you could say to make the pain better. You just had to be there for each other physically. I cried and cried until I couldn't any longer.

"Percy," I whispered.

"Shh, you can explain later. All that matters is you're okay," he said, placing a finger over my lips. I wiped my tears and lay back, prompting him to as well. But he stayed sitting up.

"Why don't you lie down too?" I asked.

"I didn't want to make you uncomfortable," he answered. I patted the bed beside me, and he lay down on his side facing me. The moonlight that shone in through the window glistened off his eyes.

"Percy, there are some things that you should know," I started. He nodded his head for me to continue, and I did. I told him everything I possibly could. I told him about what happened to Liz, the dance, my snakes, my parents—I just let everything go. He gently touched my headwrap, and for a moment, I regretted telling him anything. Normally, I would feel my snakes get restless when they felt like they were in danger. But Percy's touch was so gentle that they remained calm.

"How long have you been hiding who you are?" he asked.

"All my life." A tear streamed down my cheek.

"So, you don't even know where you came from?"

"No…but Percy, you're not scared of me?"

"What reason do I have to be scared when you saved my life?" Percy rubbed his fingers against the gauze above my wound almost like he was reminding me I had risked my life for his.

"I guess you have a good point, but still…" I said.

"You couldn't help the way you were born. None of us can, but we all do the best with what we've been given. Meadow, don't blame yourself for things that were out of your control."

"Anyone who comes close to me is always at risk, like my only childhood friend Sarah, and now Liz. There is a prophecy that states someone is going to come back to me in every lifetime and the fate of my life will always be in his hands. I am his target, and he won't stop until he finds and kills me."

"Not if we find him first." Percy winked and pulled me closer to him so my face pressed into his chest. I felt a tear stream down, but this time it wasn't a sad tear. This time it was a happy tear for finally being accepted for who I was.

CHAPTER 12

SAFE

I woke up and was still lying in his warm arms. I remembered how he changed the bandage on my chest and made no moves whatsoever on me, showing his respect for me. With every touch, he asked if it was okay. It made me feel safe to be with him. I still felt like I didn't know enough about him, though.

"Why were you in the library that day?" I asked.

"What day?" he bounced a question right back at me.

"The day I saw you sitting there looking at the Greek exhibit." I could replay that memory in my mind as if it had just happened.

"Well, why does anyone come to the museum? To explore and learn more," he said, and I could tell there was more than he revealed.

I lifted my eyebrows, and he clearly understood I was asking for more.

"Okay. I have never known my birth mother. All that was left to me were some journals about Ancient Greece, and ever since I found those entries and read them, I go to the museum to feel closer to her."

"I didn't realize. I'm sorry." I immediately felt regretful for asking, but in a way, I was glad because he opened up to me. I felt like I owed him back, but remembered how much I had already told him.

"And what brought you there?"

"Well, it's my job, silly." I winked. He pressed his hand into mine, and my fingers went up to his knuckles; he folded his fingers over each of my own.

"Can I tell you something?" I asked, thinking back to the crime scene and the prophecy.

He nodded.

"I think someone is after me, and I am scared. All my life, I have hidden who I am, but there's someone out there killing anyone and everyone who resembles me." I could feel the goosebumps creep up my arms. He seemed to feel me shiver and wrapped his arms around me tighter. "I think I am next."

"I have an idea," he said. Just then, we heard birds chirping and saw light creeping in. He talked about going back to the museum once it re-opened and acting as if everything was normal, but the only thing that would be different would be his eyes on me. Percy would come during my work hours and act as a regular attending customer.

"Don't you have a job?" I asked.

"I work nights," he answered.

"Don't you sleep?" I gasped. "Vampire. You're a vampire. That explains a lot."

"Yup, you got me. No, I mean, I can work my night shift, sleep for like seven hours and be there in time for you to head to work. I get out around twelve usually. We can make it work."

"I can't put anyone else in danger." I got up, put my shoes on, and got out of his bed. I nearly stumbled when I tried to stand, and he caught me.

"This isn't your choice, so you're not putting me in danger. Hell, I'll be there anyway at the Greek exhibit," he replied.

"Well… I should probably get your number then." I smiled, putting my hand out for him to write his number on. He stood up and got a Sharpie from his nightstand and walked back over, writing two dots on my palm. After the two dots, he made a curve underneath, and I realized he had drawn a smiley on my hand.

"What is this, the nineties?! Pull out your phone and I'll give you my number." He laughed, grabbing my phone off the nightstand and handing it to me. I took it and saw I had several missed calls from Mom. I scrolled up through the messages and finally got to the voicemails. I played the most recent one and pressed the phone to my ear.

"Your father and I love you very much. You may not have been our own, but you have become part of our family. We can't imagine a life without you in it. Honey, whatever you do, do not come home. It isn't safe here. We love you, sweetie." The line went dead.

"I have to go!" I shoved the phone into my pocket and scampered toward the door, fighting through the pain that still radiated from my chest wound. He persisted in coming with me, but I was already out the door. On the way out, I realized my car was still parked at the museum from when Percy brought me to his apartment. I had no means to get over to my parents other than using an Uber. I walked over to his car and folded my arms against my chest, knowing he would be out shortly as he knew I had no way of getting there either.

"At least let me drive you there." He walked over with his boots' laces undone and a belt not even tied completely around his waist. The sight of his disheveledness would have normally made me laugh if I weren't so worried about what I would find at home.

"Okay…but no coming in. Promise?" I put my pinky out to make him promise. He sealed it with his own.

FAMILY

Destruction. Many people focused on the physical destruction of property or land after a hurricane. Or when a tornado ripped roofs off people's houses and there wasn't much left after afterward except the quiet that followed the noisy storm and complete and utter chaos. Everything in the house was there as I had left it the night before. I urged Percy to stand back even though I knew he would find a way around the promise and come anyway. I crept into the house expecting everything to be thrown about and even some things to be missing, but was surprised to see everything in order. In fact, it appeared even cleaner than ever before. There were some sandwiches on the counter that both Mom and Dad hadn't gotten to yet. Even the butter knife she used to make them was carefully resting atop the butter. I walked over and picked it up, imagining that just a few hours before, she had been holding it herself and everything had been normal in the world. Her world, anyway. Just as I was about to lose myself completely, I could see a glimpse of Percy in the window out back. I shook my head, knowing full well he would still go out and look. Technically, he promised to stay out of the house. He didn't promise he wouldn't go on the property.

I walked closer to the window, and he gestured for me to come outside. I listened, not knowing what he could have possibly found. As soon as I opened the squeaky back door, there it was. All before me. A sign...a warning. A message.

Fate will decide.

It was spray-painted over the grass that was once so perfectly green. But now, the bright red paint that mimicked the wretched bloodiness of the crime scene I had witnessed at work was back to haunt me. My hand was over my mouth, and I felt like my feet were cemented to the ground, unable to take a step further. I thought back to the book that lay open to the story of. I knew her fate, and someone was out there trying to seal my own with one similar to hers.

"Do you hear something?" Percy snapped me out of my endless thoughts. Before I answered back, I tried to listen through the swaying trees as their branches and leaves moved with the wind. I heard murmuring as if someone were trying to say something but could find no words. I walked down the steps of the back porch and followed the rocky pathway down by the garden, then stopped to listen again. The murmuring came again, but was even louder. I was closer. When I looked over at the hatch to the basement, I felt like I was on the other side of whatever was making the sound. I quietly gestured for Percy to come here.

"But you said not to go in," he whispered obediently. I looked back into his green eyes and urgently pressed my lips onto his.

"I need you," I whispered back.

With that, he went up to the back porch and through the house, presumably down the stairs to see what was making the noise in the basement. I knew he had made it down there when the murmuring had stopped and there was just silence. I waited patiently and wondered if I should have gone in too, but knew we would have both just been sitting ducks walking into a possible trap. I heard banging coming from the other side of the metal doors that lay before me. Something or someone was clanging from the inside. I ran to the side of the house, peering out so I could see who it was before I made a run for it. Percy came out, so I felt a weight of relief come off my chest. Shortly after, Mom and Dad came out with tape still binding their hands that they were trying to peel off themselves. I ran up to the group with my arms out wide.

Percy urgently came up to me and took my hand in his before I could say anything to my parents. They seemed to be just fine with letting him take the lead.

"You all need to go. I can handle what is to come. Run...and don't look back," he said as my eyebrows furrowed in confusion.

"Mom, we can't leave him…" I said.

"We need to listen to him as he is looking out for your best interest; something your father and I have done almost your entire life. I didn't want to leave Percy there, but I was torn between him and my parents. And even if they hadn't raised me from birth, they were still my people; they were all I knew, my constants in this ever-changing world.

"Listen to him, Med," Dad urged as he clearly saw the hesitation in my eyes.

"I'll be okay. I promise." Percy crossed his fingers together and headed back in the hatch, closing the large metal doors behind him. I ran out back with both of my parents and nearly tripped over the roots of the trees that traced the earth. We could have taken the car, but decided against it, knowing it would throw off whoever was after us…whoever was after…me.

"Wait, wait," Mom and Dad were ahead of me, using their walking sticks to feel around to escape. I had gone much slower than them, reluctant to keep going since I didn't want to leave Percy behind. As soon as they got on the other side, they pressed their backs up against the side of their house, gasping for air from running so much. I did the same, but couldn't help but ask the question that had been puzzling my mind for so long.

"Meadow, not right now. We need to get as far away as possible. These people do not play around," Mom sternly said.

"Who is after me??" I asked.

"Let me say this just once." Dad walked over to me and pulled me in for a hug, resting my head on his chest. "I never thought I would say this before, but I can honestly say I am glad I couldn't see who bound us in the basement and left us there, making threats that they would be back after using us as bait to get you." Mom joined our hug, but I broke out before they could say any more.

"Percy." I felt my heart sink even further in my chest.

"If you go back there, you'll be putting both your lives at risk. It is no use now. He will be okay," Mom reassured me.

"You don't know that," I said. "I have something that could help him." I thought about my snakes and felt them squirm under my headwrap.

"Meadow," they both begged.

"I love you both. I will see you again. I promise." I started running the other way, backtracking all the way home, jumping over the roots of the trees that tripped me far too often growing up. When I rushed by the tall oak that towered over me even more when I was a little girl, I could still see the carvings I had made with rocks I found. There were three simple words that I wrote.

I am home.

I remember I wrote those words when we first moved to this house, when Mom and Dad officially adopted me. But what occurred to me that had never before was that those three words weren't about the house that we lived in at all. No...those three words referred to how I felt in my heart when I was with my loved ones. Home. I continued on, even faster than I had run before. The hatch that Percy had closed behind himself lay open. Whoever came back must have been in that very basement with him. I crept closer and decided to go inside the house to sneak into the little passage I would take whenever I was exploring the house when I was young. At every corner of the house, I peered around to make sure no one was watching or could hear me. I finally made it to the dumbwaiter and wedged myself in, pulling the string up from the top so I could make it down to the basement.

I didn't even have to open the doors as I could hear their conversation in full. But what stuck me the most was the fact they did not appear to be arguing in any way. Instead, it seemed as though they had known one another.

CHAPTER 14

THE TRUTH

"It's not like that, I swear." Percy's voice was stern. "We have to go slow and then eventually…eventually, she will be ours." I felt like I was going to vomit any second as I knew they were clearly talking about me.

"You're not thinking of the prophecy," a woman's voice came, slithering in like a snake. I felt my own grow restless and defensive. I had to pat them before they began hissing.

"Are you kidding me? Everything I do is for this prophecy. Why must it be fulfilled anyway?" he questioned the girl.

"I knew you were backing out. The girl, she has become something to you," she hissed back. Just then I felt my foot fall forward in the dumbwaiter. I quickly pulled it back in before anyone could notice. There was silence, so they must have heard me. I gulped down hard.

The silence cut like a knife. Neither Percy nor the girl said a word for several minutes until he broke the silence.

"Probably a rat or something. Look, I am just wondering what comes of this prophecy; why are we going through all of this? And to kill random people...why?"

"The prophecy is fate. If we do not obey, you know what will happen. Perseus, if you do not turn her in, and I mean her decapitated head, by sunrise tomorrow, more lives will be in your hands. Let this be your last warning," the woman threatened. I could hear her heels click against the hardwood floor and up each step until she was gone. I thought of the name she referred to him as and remembered the prophecy in detail from the book at the museum when this all seemed to have begun. I felt my snakes swarm in anger as they could feel my disappointment in the deception that I now faced. All along, Percy—or should I say, Perseus—

inserted himself in the investigation. He was the reason my boss died. The reason my parents had been tied up. From the beginning, he pretended to be my friend. But in actuality, I have never been able to keep a true friend, not since Sarah…and even then, it didn't last long. The truth of the matter was that people would keep dying until the prophecy was met, and from the book, I was meant to die by the hands of the man that was falling in love with.

I wrapped my snakes up in my headwrap and pushed myself out of the dumbwaiter, no longer wanting to hide. If I waited a moment longer, it would mean even more casualties. My life was certainly not worth the lives of many. When I pushed myself out onto the floor again, I felt a sense of relief at not having to be cooped up any longer. But that relief was soon suppressed as I saw Percy staring right at me, his green eyes piercing through me like a double-edged sword.

"Meadow," he mouthed. If it were possible, his jaw would have dropped to the ground. Instead of any malicious intent, concern filled his eyes.

"Just take me, Perseus."

He stepped toward me, and I flinched as he came closer. When I came back here, I had fully intended to save him from whatever monster that tied my parents up. I would have turned him away as I turned them to stone. Little did I realize, the only saving he needed was from himself. He didn't say any more and just walked over to the bookshelf, grabbing a composition book and pencil. He opened it up, and it appeared like he was scribbling something as quickly as he could. He picked it up and brought it over to me. Before I could protest or turn away, he put his finger over his mouth as if to tell me to be quiet. I took the notebook from him and read it.

I don't want to turn you in. They may be listening. There must be another way.

I looked up at him and put out my hand. At first, he seemed confused but realized what I was asking for and placed the pencil in my hand. I turned to the next page and pressed the notebook against the wall so that I could write on a flat surface. I gave it back to him.

I don't see another way, and the longer we wait, the more people die. Bring me in. Dead or alive. I am tired of running.

He put the book down and came closer to me. I couldn't help but back away until I was up against the wall. He brought his lips to my ear and whispered, sending a chill down my spine.

"I won't let anything happen to you," he said.

"It is out of your control," I whispered back.

"I'll figure out a way." He locked his eyes with mine for a moment longer than I could stand and pressed his lips to mine. And just then, I felt all my worries melt away for a split second. The betrayal I felt and resentment toward him washed away. Although part of me wanted to pull away, the tension in the kiss felt like a magnet that was keeping me there. Even despite its pull, I wanted to stay there for as long as I could. His soft lips parted as he pulled away, locking eyes with me, ensuring that it was okay. I nodded and put my hand on the back of his head, pushing him toward me so we could lock lips once more. It felt forbidden and like destiny all at once.

"I have a plan," he said as he pulled away. "We need to go somewhere else though. Where can we meet?"

"The library," I said. It was the first thing I could think of right away.

"You leave first, and I'll be right behind you. We'll meet there and talk about it so we don't have to worry about being watched. This is the place they would come first."

"Are you sure?" I asked.

He sealed our plans with a kiss that I never wanted to end.

CHAPTER 15

THE PLAN

It had been so long since I had been at the library. The last time I was here, everything had been perfectly normal, or so I thought. Little did I know, there was a lot going on behind the scenes. I always thought of my snakes as a curse, but never knew there was a whole prophecy behind them. Never did I realize fate would bring me where I was currently. Just a few cars filled the parking lot, but my usual spot remained untouched. I pulled in right under the shade of the weeping willow tree and looked around for Percy. He was likely waiting it out, so it didn't look too obvious in case we were being followed. Who knows, he may have even wanted to throw them off his trail. Whoever 'them' even were. Despite seeing him talk to the woman who was clearly an enemy, I felt the truth in his kiss. The passion that he pressed into my lips made the walls that I had so carefully put up out of anger and betrayal come down a little.

I finally walked into the library and headed toward the back, hoping he would find me there. After a few moments, I decided to go down a particular aisle in the library where could find me more easily. I walked past the many Greek myths of Heracles, Thanatos, Hypnos, Zeus...then I got lost down a rabbit hole in trying to find the name that was in the prophecy: Medusa. There was a whole row dedicated to that myth. Each and every one that I took out made Medusa appear as a villain with her snakes. I sympathized with her. When people cannot understand something and it's not familiar to them, they tend to banish it from existence and shun it from their communities.

"Nice find," Percy said as I nearly jumped out of my skin. I had been so immersed in the row of books I had found that I wasn't even looking out for him anymore.

"Where have you been?" I couldn't help but ask, still kneeling toward the books. He kneeled beside me and gently took the book from my hands.

"I left to come here, but felt like I was being followed, so I took a few wrong turns, changed my car and now I'm here." He looked down at the book. "What have we got here?"

"Just a villainous monster…like me." I winked, half-jokingly. Deep down, I had felt like a monster since birth. He put the book away and took my hand in his, turning his head toward the people who sat at the tables studying, procrastinating, and what have you.

"You see all those people there?" he asked. I nodded. "You wouldn't know at first glance what they are capable of doing or what they have done in their lives. There could be a murderer among us for all we know. But the point is, just because someone appears a certain way on the outside, doesn't mean they are bad."

"Hmm…murderers among us and then a sweet little pep talk. I don't know which is more comforting." I couldn't help but be playful with him, but I knew we had to start talking about what our next step was. We only had so much time.

"You're something else, you know that?" He poked me on the shoulder and got up, extending his hand for me to take so we could go do what we had intended to.

"I know just where to go," I said, continuing to hold his hand in mine as I brought him back toward the front of the library and down the stairs. Everything was bright down here, and there were signs for the children's area. Two girls were behind a makeshift stage playing with puppets. There were a few others playing with a train set and a mother reading to her baby in a rocking chair toward the back. I looked back at him, and he had an eyebrow up, showing his confusion. I laughed and continued toward the side tables that were completely open. They had small chairs, and I just about lost my mind when I watched him try to pull out the child-sized chair for himself and squeeze himself onto it. I was surprised it didn't break.

"This is the last time I let you choose a spot for us in the library," he said as he smiled, looking back at the kids who were performing their puppet play. He shook his head and brought his attention back to me.

"This is my safe place; I've come here since I was little. It's safer than upstairs, where you claimed there were 'murderers' among us," I noted.

"Okay, as you say."

"I have a notebook that I wanted to write our plan in." I pulled out the small composition book that he used to write to me when we were in the basement.

"You came prepared. Well, you may not be able to write as fast as I am dictating, but I want to explain the prophecy to you. And then, the plan. The plan won't make sense unless you know about what is fated for us." He shrugged his shoulders and I nodded, not wanting to interrupt.

"You see, in every generation there is a being with snakes for hair. She is born of sea monsters but appears human and is mortal. The sight of her snakes, even through the reflection of a mirror, has the ability to turn anyone to stone. From there, they will be frozen in place for all of eternity." He paused. "You sure you want to hear more?"

"Yes. I'm sorry; it's just weird talking about this when I have hidden the very thing you are talking about for my whole life."

"Well, you don't need to hide anymore...not from me," he reassured me. I walked over and planted a kiss on his cheek, completely forgetting about the children nearby until we both heard them gushing over the cheek kiss I gave him.

"Ooooooooh," the girls from the puppet show said. I felt my cheeks grow bright red.

"Don't you girls have prince and princess puppets that you can make live happily ever after?" Percy asked them.

"Good idea!!" they both shouted. The librarian shushed them, and they giggled quietly among themselves, scurrying to find the puppets to put on a new show together.

"If only it were that simple, no princess puppets would have snakes for hair. That would be one of the monster puppets." I sat back down in my chair, taking mental notes that he was good with kids.

"Well then, there will be another monster puppet to match her. What are we even talking about?!" He seemed to snap himself out of the looney talk, and I couldn't help but laugh.

"Okay, okay. So in the prophecy, there is also a man named Perseus. His father is the god, Zeus. However, his mother is a mortal. This makes him a demigod. In every lifetime, he must find Medusa and behead her. Many times, he does this to protect his mother or other loved ones."

"So, you're saying that I am Medusa, and you are Perseus." I put the pieces of the puzzle together. "What is your plan? I'd rather not get beheaded, but if it comes to that, so others won't be harmed, I will."

"Shh, shh, no one's going to get beheaded. What are we, in ancient Greek times?! There's another way," he said. "It has never been attempted before, but I think it might just work."

"Alright, let's hear it."

"We will need to go to the Underworld and find Hades. Once we meet him, we can strike a deal with him. He loves deals."

"Are you out of your mind?!"

"Just a little bit." He smiled.

CHAPTER 16

DON'T BACK OUT

"You seem like you've done this before." I shivered, letting him lead the way this time. We were in a rowboat that belonged to his family. The breeze made the chill that much more unbearable. He took off his sweatshirt and draped it over my shoulders.

"Oh yeah, I come out here to hang out all the time," he said sarcastically.

"I'm going to give my parents a call, so they know I'm okay," I said as I pulled out my phone.

"No!" he nearly yelped. "Turn off your location. You can tell them you're okay through text. Try to act normal. There could be a chance that there are some people watching your parents just in case you were to go there."

"Ugh, when will this ever end?"

"Soon, very soon." He continued rowing us farther and farther into the waters. The farther we went, the darker the sky grew. Ominous clouds rolled in, and the silence was broken by Percy's mumbles under his breath. I wanted to ask him what he was saying, but he seemed to be in a trance-like state. He wasn't even blinking—just staring forward and rowing as if he were a machine that couldn't stop.

Moments later, his gaze turned to me, and we locked eyes. I had a feeling he knew much more than I did as to what was about to happen, but there would have been no words to explain it anyway. All around us, the water seemed to part, and our rowboat stopped, clearly aground and unable to move any farther. He hopped out of the boat and stood on deep blackish-blue sand that had an ethereal glow to it. I took his hand and gently touched the surface of the sand, not knowing if it would swallow me whole. When I was just about to get my other leg out of the boat, I stumbled and almost fell back into the parted waters. Percy caught my fall and brought me back up to stand beside him. He looked out toward the darkness, which had a singular warm glow that escaped from it. It appeared to be moving. As it got closer to us, the warm glow became even larger until I realized it was from a lantern that dangled off the pointed edge of a wooden canoe. Behind it was a sight that I wished I could block out of my imagination, but nothing in me would have been able to do so. It was an image that would remain embedded in my mind for all eternity.

A man—a being—stood tall in the canoe that harnessed the warm glow. In his hand was a single ash-gray rod he used to guide himself forward. His entirety was swallowed by a large black cloak. The most troubling sight of all was that he had no face. Just a blank slate of pale white echoed into the darkness along with the lantern's light. I felt myself get closer to Percy and grab on to his arm, partly hiding behind him.

"He will take us to the Underworld through the River Styx. Give him this coin." He handed a gold coin to me, of which I wondered where he had even found it and remembered the stolen things from the museum. I reluctantly took the coin from him but remained behind him as the cloaked figure neared even closer to us. Just as Percy indicated, the man dug his guiding rod into the dark sands around us and put out his hand, extending his skeletal fingers.

I peered out from behind Percy and went to place the coin in the man's hand when he unexpectedly closed his hand around my own. I tugged away and realized it was no use. Somehow, the man's strength outweighed anything I could go against despite his hand being bony and his body seemingly frail.

"Tell him your name," Percy said.

"Meadow." My lip quivered as I wanted more than anything to be free of the man's grasp.

"Your true name," he said, and I hesitated at first, but remembered the prophecy.

"Medusa." Saying it out loud made it feel that much more real. As soon as the words lifted off my tongue, the man released his grasp on me and turned his head to the back of his canoe, putting his hand out as if to say we could now board.

"This is Charon. He is the one who controls the ferry that brings souls through the River Styx. He will guide us down until Cerberus sounds and then releases us to the Main Gate."

"And you know this, how?" I asked.

"I have been raised knowing this stuff my entire life. I was born studying it for when the time was right," he carefully answered, and it appeared as though he wanted to take the last part back as he covered his mouth with his hand.

"Preparing to chop my head off?"

"Yes, but things have changed. Come, let me help you." He lifted me up into the canoe and followed soon after. Right when we got into the canoe, the waters were no longer parted, and where we had once stood was now flooded. Charon turned away from us and began rowing. I was just thankful he turned away, and I didn't have to see his face any longer…or lack thereof.

"How have things changed so much when you have prepared your whole life for this?"

"Well, you've studied Greek mythology or at least seen a lot of it after working at the museum. So you must know all the wars and battles that had been fought over love."

"You must be crazy."

"Not the answer I was expecting." He smirked.

The silence was replaced by a howl that crept closer and filled my stomach with butterflies. I knew full well what was to come. Cerberus—the three-headed dog. The closer we seemed to come, the more the howls turned into growls. The dogs were sniffing us out and could tell we were intruders who didn't belong here. I looked over at Percy, and he pulled out another stolen artifact from the museum: Orpheus's lyre. The gold shimmered and reflected against the river.

"Follow my lead, okay?" He began strumming a slow melody that reminded me of the bedtime lullabies my mom would sing for me so I could fall asleep. The howling ceased, and Charon pulled the canoe against the edge of land. Percy continued playing as he got up and stepped off, signaling for me to do the same. I followed him, still cautious about the dogs. There was a clear pathway that led all the way to a stone archway that I assumed was the Main Gate to the Underworld. When I looked behind me, Charon was gone. I felt a chill down my spine as I wondered if he was still there somewhere in the darkness or picking up other lost souls that were doomed to an eternity in the Underworld.

When Percy and I came up to the gate, the three dogs were sleeping, and drool pooled out of one of their mouths. My heart was racing because I realized at any moment, the giant dogs could wake up and devour both of us. We crept past the gate and, as soon as we were in, the metal bars came down from the entryway, closing us in completely. Percy stopped playing the lyre and placed it in his bag, of which I wondered what else he possibly had in there. There were three directions that the pathway forked into. On the left was the judgment pavilion, in the middle was Hades' palace and on the right was the entrance to Tartarus. The palace reminded me of Mount Olympus and the Parthenon. There was a giant hill on which a building resembling the Parthenon stood, overlooking the Underworld.

"We must go right to Hades' palace. There is no time to waste," Percy said.

"And what will we even say?" I asked. "How can we stop this prophecy so I don't end up beheaded?"

"Exactly."

We continued down the middle pathway, which brought us to another path that inclined up the mountain, going around again and again until we'd reached the top. It was the tallest mountain I had ever had to climb and felt like it would take forever. On the side of one boulder, there was room to climb. I decided to take the faster route rather than continuing the endless roundabout. Percy gave me a boost, and I was able to reach the next rock to continue climbing. There were three more stepping stones until I finally found myself at the top. I lay flat on the dirt before the palace, looking up toward the sky of the Underworld, which was riddled with endless storms, lightning bolts crashing, and darkness. It hadn't appeared this way until we reached the top. I felt my snakes slither restlessly, and I felt their pain. I, too, wanted a sense of familiarity or to just go back home and hide. If I made it out of the Underworld alive, I would consider myself lucky.

CHAPTER 17

PALACE OF HADES

"Need a hand there?" an ominous voice came from above as I struggled to get myself up. Percy lay beside me, but I knew the voice was from someone else. I lifted myself up and saw a tall, muscular man with a black chiton covering half of his legs and extending over half of his torso, draped over his left shoulder. His wavy dark hair went down to his shoulders, and he had red eyes that pierced my soul. I got up on my own. Percy was already standing by the time I got up.

"Good, because I wasn't going to give you one anyway," the man that I presumed was Hades continued sarcastically. He walked away from us and didn't look back, but seemed to know exactly what we were there for. "Let's get on with it. Follow me, and we'll do our negotiations…"

"Should we go?" I whispered to Percy.

"You came this far, that would be silly, wouldn't it?" Hades answered before Percy could. When I looked over at Percy, he just shrugged his shoulders.

"He has a point." Percy proceeded to go ahead of me and followed Hades into the entrance of his palace. Twisted vines aligned with thorns weaved in and out of the columns that held the palace up. When we entered, the floor was completely made of marble, which made it even colder and more somber than it would have otherwise been. On the right and left were skeletal soldiers holding various weapons. Their sunken and hollowed-out eyes somehow penetrated just at the very glance at them. When I had thought Charon was frightening, I had no idea of what was to come next. There was a colossal throne that had a black wing coming out from either side. The velvet cushion that lined it was a deep royal blue and seemed misplaced, but then I remembered how Hades strove to be the king of something and was placed in the Underworld according to stories I had read. He sat up on his throne and crossed his arms.

"So…let me guess. You two lovebirds are trying to figure a way out of your fate and destiny?" Hades plucked a thorn from a vine that went around his throne and started picking his teeth with it. I shuttered. But how did he know what we wanted? Had he known all along that we were coming to him from the moment we went in the rowboat?

"Lovebirds?" I asked.

"I call it like I see it," he replied. I glanced over at Percy, who was red in the face.

"We need to find a way to break the prophecy," Percy said, brining us back on topic. "There must be some way."

"What's in it for me?" Hades asked, typical. Of course, he would have been looking to strike some sort of deal.

"My snakes," I blurted out before I could think further on it. I felt them hiss under my headwrap. He got off his throne and walked over to me, extending a long, skinny finger at the top of my headwrap. I closed my eyes, unsure of what he was going to do. I could feel him trace each snake until one must have slithered out slightly and bit the edge of his finger. He jumped back and laughed.

"Ah, yes. The curse of the snakes. But what would I do with a bunch of dead snakes after I cut them off your head? I don't think they'd even serve a purpose other than a nice memento to put on display in my palace." He walked over to the table beside his throne. "Could look good here."

"You are insane," I said. I felt like I had betrayed my snakes by offering them to this lunatic.

"One tends to go insane when in the Underworld for too long." He winked and turned to Percy.

"Look, you seem like a nice guy. I knew when you were born, along with the many others in Zeus's lineage. He was just as excited to see you live out your destiny. But there is no breaking of prophecies. It's just a no-no even from me, as much as I love breaking rules that Zeus put into place."

"Let's just go. He can't help us." I tugged at Percy's arm, wanting to get out of there as soon as possible. The entire trip was a waste, and we still didn't know what to do. I would have to turn myself in. That was the only way. Percy firmly stayed put and refused to give way to my tugging.

"There's something he's not telling us," he said.

"Clever." Hades smirked. "You will not like what I have to say, especially if you two plan to be lovebirds and live happily ever after."

"Let's hear it." I was growing impatient.

Hades walked away from us and toward his skeletal soldiers. He snapped his fingers, and they seemed to do as he directed them. It was almost like he was putting on a performance with them.

"Two people fall in love, but these two are also enemies in every era of time." Two of the soldiers aimed their arrows at one another, then took each other's hands in the next second. "One has been born with a curse that is as old as time. The other must behead her to seal both of their fates." Just then one of the soldiers pulled out a machete and severed the spinal cord of the other, popping his skull off and onto the ground.

"But in order for the cursed one to live, the very opposite must happen," he continued, walking toward the beheaded skeleton soldier and placing its head back on its body. "The cursed one must use her curse on the other, sealing his fate by freezing him in time as a stone statue."

And with that, the other soldier stood still like a statue. Hades snapped his fingers, and the skeletal soldiers walked back to their line and got in formation, once again standing still, but this time they all turned toward us. I looked over at Percy and shook my head, knowing exactly what the other option would have to be. There was no way I was going to let that happen. I wouldn't be able to live with myself. But then I thought about it from Percy's perspective. He would have to live with himself after beheading me. Either way, we would both suffer. There had to have been some other way.

"Thank you for your help," Percy said despite Hades' lack thereof. I wondered why he was so polite to him when any word out of his mouth just got on my nerves. He chuckled and toyed with people's lives for fun.

"Oh, and when you come next time, try not to stay so long!" he called out from his throne. His soldiers surrounded us from behind, pushing us out of his palace. Before we knew it, we were back at the edge of the mountain that overlooked the Underworld.

I looked at Percy, and he just stared back at me. I could feel the helplessness in his heart because it matched my own.

ONE WAY OUT

The moment we stepped out of the underworld, the brightness nearly blinded me. I had to cover my eyes to let them adjust more slowly and feel around to see where I was going. I felt a hand touch mine, and I took it, knowing it was Percy's. We got all the way back to the car and sat in silence. I knew he was thinking the same thing I had been. One of us had to go, and it would clearly be me as I was the monster and would never risk Percy's life for my own. I knew he wouldn't give up without a fight though, so I had to walk right into the trap without him knowing. It wasn't yet nightfall, so I turned the key in the ignition and started driving with him in the passenger seat. To my surprise, he still said nothing. I thought he'd ask where we were going or spark up another plan, but no.

Dead silence.

I had my mind set, and there was only one place left to go. A place I went when I felt I had nowhere else to turn. A place where I never felt judged or belittled. A place where I felt at home.

I pulled into the beach parking lot and looked over at Percy. He looked down at his feet, barely seeming to notice where we were.

"If you want to stay in the car, you can. I'll leave the keys on the seat. I just need to be here right now," I said.

"Oh." He snapped out of the daze he was in and looked at the keys I just set down beside him. "Thanks, I'll be out soon."

"Cheer up, we'll figure this out."

"I should be the one cheering you up," he replied.

"You've done plenty of that. We don't have much time left, so why don't we enjoy it?" I asked.

"You definitely have a point there," he said. "Alright, alright. I'm coming!" He got out of the car and handed me my keys so I could lock the car. I dropped them to the bottom of my purse, not worrying about being able to find them later. I could already hear the waves crashing on the shore.

"I've never been here before. Where are we? This is not exactly the place to come in the dead of winter." He brought up a fairly good point.

"Took you long enough to ask. This is a place that I've been coming to since I was young. It's actually the place that the foster home first found me—almost as if I was washed up from the waves. I was found on the shore."

"You're lucky you didn't drown." He crossed his arms.

"For as long as I can remember, the water has always been my constant and a place I could go to when I needed to get away."

We both came up to the very edge of the shore where the water met the sand, except the sand was completely covered in snow. Somehow, I still felt warm despite the cold. Whenever I was beside Percy, I never felt cold. I kneeled, dipping my fingers in the water, then looked back at Percy. He was just looking out in the distance, but appeared much calmer than before. I wished this were a normal day at the beach, where we could both enjoy one another. But it might have been the last time we were together if we couldn't figure a way out of the prophecy. If this was my last day, I wanted to do everything I possibly could and leave here with no regrets.

"If only we could go in." I reminisced about the summers that I wouldn't have to worry about bundling up and the water was a sanctuary out of the heat.

"I may have something that could help." He reached into his bag. I could immediately see a shimmer of something reflecting against the water. When he pulled it out, I realized it was a golden cup of some sort. It looked like it was possibly another artifact among the many that had gone missing from the museum. But as soon as he brought it out, I felt even warmer. So warm that the snow around us instantly melted, and I could see the sand that had been hidden underneath.

"What in the world is that?! No wonder I always feel warm next to you." I nearly jumped out of my shoes.

"Have you ever heard of Helios?" he asked.

"The Sun god?"

He nodded.

"This belongs to him. It is said that he used this to travel the seas at night. It was specially crafted for him by Hephaestus."

"And it will just keep us warm just like that?" I asked.

"Just like that." He winked.

I took my shoes off, throwing them farther inland, and they clunked down in the sand. I wasn't worried about anyone running off with them because no one else in their right mind was at the beach right after snowfall.

"What are you doing?!" He laughed at my silly behavior.

"Take your shoes off," I said. "Come on, just do it."

"Okay, okay," he said and followed my lead. I took his hand and led him into the water. He set the cup down just out of the reach of the water, but heat radiated from it. Surprisingly, the water was already warm too. As soon as I traveled just far enough away from the golden cup, the cold overwhelmed the entirety of my being. I screamed and swam back toward the shallow part of the sea. Seaweed floated throughout the water, reminding me of the tangled mess my snakes must have been under my headwrap. I had been wearing a white top and black pants, so you could now fully see through my shirt down to my bra. It didn't matter. At this moment, I just simply wanted to be.

"We probably should have brought our bathing suits," he said. "Hindsight…"

"What's the fun in that?" I asked.

He splashed water at me. I splashed him right back and screamed when he made an even bigger splash.

"Stop, stop!" I put both hands up, declaring a truce. He put both of his arms down and nodded. A second later, I started splashing as much as I could as payback.

"What happened to 'stop, stop?!'" he said, laughing as he walked toward me. I tried to swim away and wasn't fast enough as he enveloped his arms around my waist and picked me up so I couldn't splash any longer.

"Well, this isn't very fair."

"And that was?!" he asked.

"Okay, you're right. I played a little dirty right there," I answered. "I'll stop."

"How can I trust that?"

"Because I have to do something."

"And what's that?"

"If you let me down, I'll show you," I answered, growing impatient of being held up in the air.

"Okay, I'll let you go, but...if you try something again, you'll wish you didn't," he said.

"Ooh, that's making me curious as to what would happen, but there's something more important that I must do."

He put me back down in the water. By now with high tide, it was going up to our shoulders, but we were still able to stand on the ocean floor. I put my hand under his chin and brought his face forward so we were staring into one another's eyes. Without being able to stand a second longer, I pressed my lips against his. He put his hand on the back of my head, pressing against the snakes. His touch seemed to calm them as they didn't protest in the slightest. I continued kissing him, pulling away only to breathe. I felt his tongue make its way into my mouth, and I brushed mine against his. His other hand remained underwater and pressed against the small of my back. He guided his fingers up to my breasts and traced my nipples with his fingers. The more he touched me, the more passionate our kisses grew.

"Can I spend the night with you?" I asked.

"On one condition," he said. "You kiss me like you just did again."

I nodded, and we raced back toward the car, tagging one another on the way back as if we were little kids again and life was simple. When we finally got there, he told me he'd give directions to his place. I was curious what it was like and whether he had any roommates. I felt like he knew a lot about me, but I didn't know enough about him. No matter where we went, I knew I wanted to finish what we had started as soon as I possibly could.

CHAPTER 19

BENEATH HIM

He brought me to his childhood home, which looked abandoned. There were no cars in the driveway except for the one we took to get there. The lights were completely off in the house, and vines were growing over the windows. He parked the car and walked around to my side, but I just sat there in disbelief. I couldn't even imagine what it looked like on the inside.

"This is where you stay?" I asked.

"God, no. This is just my childhood home." He smiled. "Be careful. Don't judge her too harshly."

"Never," I promised, taking his hand and stepping out onto the driveway that had weeds protruding from the various cracks within the pavement. He brought me up the steps to the front door and pulled out a key from a groove in the step.

"What if someone found that?" I couldn't help but ask. It was such an obvious hiding spot.

"Then they'd be in for a surprise on the other side," he said, opening the door and placing his arm inside, then jumping back. "Duck!" I followed what he said, and in the next second, an arrow came flying out from inside. Behind us, it targeted right in the center of a nearby oak tree. On the ground below, there was a pile of arrows that must've been from other times he visited.

"A trap?!" I hesitated going any farther, but saw the look in Percy's eyes urging me to follow him in. I followed. As soon as we got in, he shut the door behind us. The hardwood floor was sparkling as if someone had just cleaned it. There was a black piano in the corner of the room, which also looked brand new. What was most striking was the lack of electronics and no TV. Usually, a living room space housed a television at the very least and couches right in front of it. But instead, there was just a piano and a dining table with various chairs and place settings already done as if company were about to come any second.

I walked over to the piano and sat down, looking over to Percy for the okay. I felt as though I were in a museum and couldn't touch anything. It was all too perfect. I rested my fingers on the keys and found the ones I remembered from playing long ago. I started to play the melody of a song I last played for my parents. The gentle stroke of the keys revealed the song to Percy as he came closer and began singing the lyrics to "Can't Help Falling In Love."

I stood up and looked him dead in the eyes, knowing full well I wanted to finish what we had started, but I had so many questions lingering. I also wanted to see more of the house.

"Meadow," he called to me as I was walking over to the table to inspect that too. I turned around and stayed quiet as he looked like he had more to say.

"None of this is your fault," he said. "I just want you to know that."

"Have you ever met anyone like me with the curse that I have? Probably not. The only thing my curse can do is kill others. So, how is this not all my fault?" I couldn't help but ask.

"Come," he said. "I have one more thing to show you."

I followed him down a long hallway. There were several rooms on either side, but the doors remained shut. He brought me all the way to the very last one and opened the door slowly, revealing a perfectly normal bedroom. Deep-blue walls surrounded us as soon as I stepped in. There were star stickers along the walls that glowed in the dark. As the sun was just setting, barely any light came into the room. I heard Percy click a button, and a light came on in the corner of the room. It wasn't just any light, though. It projected the constellations onto the walls. He sat at the edge of his bed and patted the spot beside him to prompt me to sit down too.

"This is what we see in the sky, and do you want to know what is special about that to you and me specifically?" he asked.

"What?"

"In every lifetime that we come back to pursue our destiny, it is and always will be under these same stars. No matter how many times you have lost your life to this prophecy, you will always come back under the same night sky with the same stars glowing evermore."

"I never thought of it that way," I said, looking at one specific star that seemed to glow the brightest on his wall. "I guess that's because I hadn't even known until recently about the prophecy."

He turned to face me and took my hands in his.

"No matter what, it's going to turn out okay. Let's take a word from your playbook and enjoy whatever's left of the time we do have."

"Okay, but I have questions." I stood up.

"Go ahead." He stayed where he was on the edge of the bed.

"Where is everyone? Why is this house abandoned?" I asked.

"They took my mother away until I fulfill the prophecy."

"What?? Is she okay?!"

"She's fine. Remember, this happens every lifetime to us. It's a cycle that will continue to repeat. Remember, this is *not* your fault."

"So you keep the house clean for the moment she finally does come home?"

"Yeah. I have always hoped I could do it without hurting anyone."

"Okay, next question…"

"Keep them coming," he said.

I paced back and forth on this one. I was trying to think of how to word it the right way without coming off too harsh, but decided to just ask with whatever words I could find.

"When you came to the museum, were you there to fulfill the prophecy right there and then?" I asked.

"Do you want the long answer or short?"

"Whichever."

"Short answer, yes. I came there to behead you, but had been there long before. I just didn't know it was you who was the other part of the prophecy. I needed some tools, which is why many artifacts had gone missing. Also, before you ask, I did not murder your boss. That was done by the overseer of this prophecy, the woman I was speaking to in the basement of your place—she has my mother captive."

"And…long answer?"

"Long answer is that from the moment I sat down and pretended not to watch you, any hatred or blame I had built up in my mind for you had quickly diminished. Despite what you think, you are not a monster at all. It's humans who are the true monsters. I mean, look at all that is happening in the world. When I looked at you, I could see how pure you were and untouched by the spread of humanity's cruel ways. You handled your job with such care and your coworkers with such loyalty. The long answer was that I fell in love with you from the moment I laid my eyes on you, and I have been trying to buy us time since then."

"Percy," was all I could say. He put out his arms and gently grasped my hands in his, pulling me back toward the bed. I straddled him, pushing him down the width of the bed. I met his lips with my own and began kissing down his neck, feeling him shiver the more I touched him. He wrapped his arms around me and rolled over so he was on top, and I lay there staring up at him, barely able to keep my eyes open. I felt as though I were in a state of ecstasy as my eyes constantly rolled to the back of my head. My toes curled, and I knew I wanted more.

"I want you." He took the words right out of my mouth.

"Have me."

As soon as those two words escaped my tongue, it seemed he turned into a savage animal. He tore my shirt off and started kissing down my breasts and stomach. I pushed off my pants as he did the same with his and gently pushed into me. With each thrust, I felt like my mind was blown. I held on to his shoulders, digging my nails in the faster he went. He stifled my moans with his lips as he kissed me repeatedly. In the next second, he picked me up and held me against the wall, continuing to push into me again and again. I was helpless in his arms and completely submissive and vulnerable in every way. He brought me back to the bed and lay down beside me. I wanted more than anything to please him any way I could, so I straddled him, pushing him into me once more. I slowly pushed my body closer to him and retreated again until finally he seemed to not be able to take anymore and grabbed on to my waist, thrusting his hips up into mine. With a sudden stop, he put his hand on the back of my head and pushed my lips into his, exhaling excessively. I rolled over beside him and let out a huge breath.

"Why did it take us so long to do that?" I joked.

"You took the words right out of my mouth." He smiled and turned toward me. His eyes looked like they were growing heavier and heavier by the minute until silence encapsulated the room and we both drifted to sleep.

TURN YOURSELF IN

The next morning, I woke up and had forgotten where I was at first. After being chased out of my childhood home, stopping at the apartment, visiting the Underworld, and entering Hades' Palace—I no longer knew whether I was coming or going anymore. I turned to find Percy lying there beside me in his bed from his abandoned childhood home. He lay there looking so peaceful. It almost reminded me of when we first met in the museum and how, to me anyway, I felt much more carefree at the time. His dark eyelashes brushed against the top of his cheeks, and I had to stifle a laugh because of how bad his bed head was. It was almost like in those cartoons when someone would touch an electric socket and their hair would stick up from being electrocuted.

I slowly moved out from under the sheets and replaced where I had been lying with a pillow. I could hear the birds chirping and realized it was morning, which meant it was only a matter of time before I had to turn myself in. That is what I had decided on; it was the only thing that made sense at this point. If not for Hades' failed attempt at a negotiation or lack thereof, things could have been different. But this prophecy was one that neither of us could escape, in any lifetime.

I had left the room intending to leave, but realized I had no way to get to where I needed to go. We seemed to be in a forest in this abandoned home, and I hadn't the slightest clue how long it would take me to get back. Car keys. Trying my best not to wake Percy, I put my hand in his jacket pocket that lay on the ground beside him. A slight jingle sounded, and I knew I had found them. I looked up, frantic that the sound had woken him. It reminded me of Cerberus and how we had to lull the dogs to sleep. His eyes were still closed, but he exhaled and stretched, then rolled over to the other side where I had placed the pillow. He wrapped his arms around the pillow, and I wondered if he had thought it was me in his sleep. He was a silly man who made me laugh, and I wished I had more time with him. There was no time to waste, though. If he woke up and I was still there, he would've done everything in his power to keep me from walking right back into the trap that had been laid out for me.

I walked out the back door, not wanting to test the trap out front with an arrow that could potentially go right through me. When I got to the driveway, I took one last look at the abandoned house and imagined what it must have looked like when Percy's mother was still there. I imagined all the memories they must have shared in this house. Playing the piano. Running around in the yard. Normal things that normal people did. That's when I knew my decision to turn myself in was the right choice all along. I was the only outlier. I only wished we didn't have to both endure this dreadful fate every lifetime.

I turned the key in the ignition and knew the sound had to have woken Percy. I quickly put my home address into my phone and peeled out of the driveway as if I were a cast member of *The Fast and Furious*. The tires squealed as I pulled out, and I continued on down the road, realizing my childhood home had actually not been too far away from his. All along, we had practically been neighbors living in the same neighborhood. I felt bad that I had left him carless, but knew it was for the best. A few minutes later, I was pulling into my driveway. There was a car already there, and I could tell it was likely the woman who Percy had been speaking to. I put the car in park and grabbed my phone to send out one last text before I would never be able to text again. I scrolled through my missed messages from Mom and Dad and clicked on Dad's name. He was always the more sensitive of the two, and I knew it would get to Mom, too. They would have the messages read aloud to them through voice texting. I clicked on the record button and saw the red line waiting to pick up my voice.

"I love you," was all I could muster up to say. I wasn't able to find any other words. There were no other words. If I were given time to say one last thing in my life, that was it. Those three words. They encompassed everything I felt, and I was saying it to some of the most important people in my life. I only wished I had said it to Percy before it was too late.

I left my phone in Percy's car and the keys on the hood of the car. I wouldn't be needing either of those things. The garden was kept full from when Mom and I had planted various types of flowers. I had never been one to garden, but she somehow kept them alive. I could barely keep a cactus alive. Upon walking in, there were more people than I had expected. Mom and Dad were both sitting at the kitchen table, and they didn't seem to be restrained in any way. Across from them was a woman I had never met before, but she didn't seem too intimidating, which confused me at first.

"Mom, Dad. Who is this?" I asked.

"Honey, you shouldn't have come home," Dad said. I could tell he was trying to hold himself together the best he could.

"What's going on?" I asked in a different way.

"This is Percy's mom, Danae..." Mom answered my first question. Before I was able to respond, a woman came out from the shadows of the hallway and laughed. If I were looking for intimidation, she gave it to me and then some. The woman was not just any woman. I could tell she was definitely not human by her large black wings that protruded from her back. She had a glowing red dress on, and her eyebrows furrowed. Her hair was black, but with a red glow to it. Along her pale arms were markings that reminded me of henna tattoos, except they were all red and matched her dress. Around her neck was a choker necklace that had a black jewel at the end of it.

"Perfect timing. The whole crew is almost here." She winked. I flinched and went to take my headwrap off and remembered Percy's mom was right there, so she wouldn't be protected.

"Ahhh, I would not do that if I were you. It would have no effect on me because I am a Greek goddess. Danae though…not so much."

"Who are you?" I had a feeling I already knew, but didn't want to assume. Based on the troublemaker ways and bitterness, I could tell she was the goddess of Discord and Strife.

"Eris. I am here to make sure the prophecy is carried out as it should be."

"Weren't you responsible for the Trojan War?" I remembered that tidbit of history and tried to delay her long enough. But then remembered, for what? I was there to turn myself in.

"You could say that. Anyway, let's not distract ourselves from the main issue. We're here to finally carry out the prophecy."

"I'm not fighting you. Take me. Do whatever you need. Just leave everyone else out of it."

"You can't do that, Meadow!" Dad shouted. Eris snapped her fingers, and tape bound his lips.

"Quite the chatterbox he is, huh?" she asked, walking toward me.

"Let them go. Take me. Behead me," I submitted.

"Oh, if it were only that simple." She put her hand under my chin and held my face in her hand. It was surprising how gentle her touch was given how intimidating she was otherwise.

"Why isn't it?" I asked.

"The prophecy states that Perseus must be the one to behead you. Not me. Not Zeus. No one else in this kingdom."

"Who made this prophecy?" Danae finally spoke up, reminding me she was even in the room with us. Eris snapped again, and she, too, had tape over her mouth. She snapped once more, and Mom was no longer able to speak either.

"People…always so curious, and where does their curiosity take them? No place good, but they will never learn, will they? That is humanity. Mistakes. Error. Clumsiness." She walked away and looked out the window.

"Just in time." She smiled. "Perseus must be the one to behead you because that is what is stated. From the beginning of time, this is how it has been, now and forever."

"He won't do it," I urged.

"Yeah, I thought about that too. But I brought a little motivation for him." She eyed his mother, who sat there with tears streaming down her cheeks and onto the tape that covered her mouth.

"Isn't there any other way?"

"If there were, I wouldn't tell you anyway." She moved her hand to the left, and it seemed to control me to the point I was no longer standing but sitting in a chair that was placed in the middle of the kitchen, right before everyone. She wanted this to be a show. And our parents would be the audience for this sick and twisted play that she would direct. It was one thing to die for those you loved, but to die in front of their eyes relinquished any comfort whatsoever that they would be okay. For the rest of their lives, they would never be able to erase this from their memories. They would be haunted for the rest of their lives.

CHAPTER 21

SACRIFICE

"Eris." Percy pushed in the door so hard it practically came off the hinges.

"Better late than never," Eris replied, calm in a room full of chaos. "Shall we get right to it?"

"No. You are holding a grudge, and the only thing you seek is revenge. Meadow didn't mean it."

"Didn't mean it? You can say that about someone breaking a pencil, accidentally spilling something on your shirt, but killing someone? Oops, sorry. I killed the love of your life. Well, this time it's going to be an eye for an eye." Eris walked over to me and crossed her hands over her chest. I couldn't help but squint, unknowing as to what she could have been talking about. Then it struck me—the dance.

"You were there?" I asked.

"To watch the horrors unfold as you turned everyone to stone? I was not only there, but I had to endure seeing the man that I had been falling in love with turn to stone right before my eyes. It would have been a far better fate to have also turned to stone with him. But watching it...that was the worst torture I have ever had to go through."

"I would explain everything, but you wouldn't even believe me," I sighed and put my head down in my hands. "I am the monster that you say I am. And no one else deserves to go through any more pain."

Percy walked over to me and kneeled beside where I sat. He took my hands in his and kissed me gently. When he got back up, he walked over to his mother and turned back to Eris.

"Fix this," he said, gesturing to his mother's taped mouth.

"They were so annoying, though," she protested. He gave her another look. "Ugh, fine," she snapped her fingers, and Percy's mother as well as my own parents no longer had tape covering their mouths. My mother was the first to speak.

"You can't mean that our Meadow killed someone. She's harmless. She wouldn't even hurt a housefly," she said. Eris just chuckled and shot a glaring look at me.

"Wow, she seems to have been able to play the role really well. This whole time, you all have believed her to be normal when she is actually quite the contrary. Do you remember a dance that you brought her to where a great tragedy occurred? And she was one of the few survivors? Did you ever think it was any coincidence she just so happened to be present and remained unscathed from whatever threat occurred?" she said. "She has the power to kill you all right this instant. A great power that no one but a god or goddess should hold."

"Meadow, what is she talking about?" Mom asked.

"She is right. I was born with a curse, but you both had accepted me almost my entire life. Your home, our home, was the one place I had felt I belonged."

"Can't you just let her go?" she asked.

"I'm done with all the talking. Percy, you are either going to fulfill your end of the prophecy or you know exactly what collateral damage will have to occur."

He silently put his hand on his mother's cheek and gave her a hug, whispering something in her ear. As soon as he pulled away, I could see the tears as they continued to stream down her face.

"No, Percy, no," she wailed, grabbing on to him.

"It is the only way."

"What is he talking about?" I asked. Before I could say anymore, the next few seconds happened so fast.

"Close your eyes," was all he said when he walked over to me, leaving his mom wailing in the back while Eris continued laughing. I thought he was talking to me as I took one last look at his green eyes and closed my own, hoping that whatever the afterlife was for me, I still had the memory of him there to replay in my mind forever. I expected to feel pain, but instead, felt nothing.

Suddenly, the laughing stopped. I heard hissing and felt my snakes squirm about on my head. The only other time they had ever been this agitated was that night at the dance. I opened my eyes to find Percy there in front of me. But this Percy was much different. My heart sank as I stared at the stone statue that stood before me. And then I realized all too fast that this had been his plan all along: to sacrifice himself for the one he loved. This was the only other way, according to Hades. Percy had pulled off my headwrap and revealed my snakes, killing himself so he could let me live. Changing our timelines forever.

CHAPTER 22

HOPE

Gone. There was something about that word that was hypocritical. Gone, but in what way? No matter what you believe in for the afterlife or even if you don't believe in one, there is one thing that is for certain: Matter can neither be created nor destroyed. So, whether you think that someone just ceases to exist when they are "gone," they just don't exist in the way they had. They exist in a different way. Percy's stone-cold body stood before me, and in that second, I wanted to rip my snakes off my head and toss them in the fireplace to burn. But I knew they didn't ask for this fate, either. Percy's mother continued to sob, while my parents were completely quiet despite not having the tape over their mouths any longer. I was unsure whether they were quiet because they were scared of me now or if they just didn't know what to say. I expected Eris to be laughing, but couldn't find her when I looked about the room. I grabbed the headwrap and placed it around my head once again, protecting the others.

I got up and went out the front door to find that Eris had just taken off, fully extending her wings as she left the ground and flew through the sky. She seemed to notice my presence and turned her head. This time, she didn't give a sarcastic wink. Instead, I could see the regret all over her face. She continued on, disappearing in the clouds up above. A true coward.

When I went back in, Percy's mother sat where I had been sitting, right in front of him. She had her arms wrapped around the statue, sobbing into its arm. The guilt weighed on my shoulders. I should have been the one that was 'gone,' not him. I walked beside her, but kept my distance, not knowing if she blamed me for this. I expected yelling, anger, ridicule, but what I got was an open hand. Danae had turned to me and was expecting me to place my hand in hers. I was unsure of why. Was she seeking revenge on me for killing her son? Whatever the case may be, I placed my hand down, and she weakly pulled me closer to her.

"My son," she said through choked up tears, "was happiest when he found you."

"He was?" I was taken by surprise. She looked up at me with those green eyes, and for a moment, I felt like I was looking through Percy's eyes.

"He would constantly go to the museum, and his excuse? To research. But I knew. I knew in those eyes, he had found a girl and had fallen in love."

"But you were taken away by Eris when he came to the museum, right?"

"This was before Eris and the prophecy. We had known of a prophecy, but he had found you even before that."

"How did he find me?" I felt bad for asking more questions, but knowing more about Percy made me feel like he was living on that much more. Danae shakily stood up and took both my hands in hers, looking over at the statue that Percy had turned into and back at me.

"It is a mystery, but they say when two souls are meant to be together, they will continue to find one another no matter what. I believe you will find him again."

"Thank you." I couldn't hold back any longer and felt a tear stream down my cheek, followed by another, and then another until I was sobbing as Danae had just been. I felt Danae's arms around me and then even more as my parents hugged me too. When I had assumed guilt for all of this, I realized that those who loved me were still by my side and always would be. No matter what. They would see the light in the darkness, even in the darkest of nights.

"There has to be a way to get him back," I said as they released me from the hug. When I walked over to him, I wished I could see those green eyes again. I wished I had taken more time to enjoy them, but instead we were both so busy trying to figure a way out of the prophecy. I pressed my hand to his cold cheek and felt that if I wasn't gentle enough, I'd make the entirety of his being crumble to pieces. Soon, darkness encapsulated the room and something fell to the ground from up above. Light came in again, but something was strange about how fast it had happened. I looked over at my parents and then Danae, and they all had the same confused look on their faces that I perceived I had as well.

I went around them and opened up the front door again. Before I could go out to see what was going on, Eris and her black wings stood before me. I wondered if she was back to finish me off since that is what she wanted in the first place. She gave me a stern look and headed back inside, walking circles around Percy.

"He is my half brother, you know," she said.

"It's shocking what you would do to your own family," I replied, wishing she would leave.

"Like I knew he would do this," she scoffed. "I am here to bring him up with me," she said, placing an arm around his waist and carrying his statue under her arm as if he were a briefcase.

"Can't you let us grieve?" Danae moaned, gesturing to take Percy back from Eris.

"Where are you taking him?" I asked, not totally ignoring what Danae had said, but genuinely curious as to what she planned to do with his body.

"You're coming with me."

"Coming where?" I stood firm, feet planted on the ground.

"Mount Olympus." Eris walked out the front door as quickly as she had come in and effortlessly lifted herself off the earth and back up into the sky. I watched as she went and wondered what was next. I wondered what could possibly be on Mount Olympus and how I would get there. In the next second, I found myself floating in the air, unable to control my body in the slightest. I caught up with Eris as we ascended higher and higher into the clouds. The mainland disappeared from view, and hope lingered on the horizon.

CHAPTER 23

MOUNT OLYMPUS

The skies turned from light blue to a peachy pink hue above the clouds. It gave an ethereal glow that made me feel like I was dreaming. The only things in the distance that reminded me of all that had happened were the dark wings that I followed. I saw the tips of Percy's stone-cold toes, and my sunken heart could never come out from where it had plummeted down to in just a few hours. Mist suddenly filled the air, and just beyond the clouds was a giant waterfall flowing down from what appeared to be the 'heavens' as people on earth would refer to it. To the right and left of the waterfall was rock beneath a colossal island. The land was the greenest I had ever seen in my life. Atop this mountain, from which the water streamed down from was what appeared to be a structure with many white columns. I looked toward Eris and saw that she was heading to a gate that stood right before the castle-like building.

"Welcome to Mount Olympus." She turned to me and smiled. I still didn't trust that smile, but she was holding something that was very dear to me under her wing. I continued following her until she flew over to a man who appeared to be the gatekeeper and gestured for me to come beside her. Her gesture seemed to control me to the point of moving me against my will. I was right at her side as she wished.

A large man walked over. His skin glowed and radiated heat. I had never seen a man so muscular in my life. He wore gold armor that shimmered in the sun, and his blue eyes seemed soft against the rest of his body.

"What kind of trouble did you get yourself into now?" The man looked at Eris and the statue of Percy and then over at me.

"Heracles, just let us in," Eris said.

"Is that Perseus?" Heracles asked.

"It was me," I admitted, breaking the silence. "I turned him to stone."

"Let's not get into the long, sappy story. Just open up the gate." She gave me a look and squinted her eyes at Heracles as if to make an unspoken threat.

"As you wish. And do you want her coming in with you?" He gestured over to me.

"Oh no, I just led her all the way here to come for the ride. Yes, let her in! I need to fix the mess I made."

Heracles rolled his eyes and pulled down on a large gold rope. With each tug, the gate opened out toward us. I backed up and watched what Eris did so I could follow her lead. The last thing she had said seemed to race circles through my mind. 'Fix the mess I made.' Would she be able to help Percy? Would she bring him back? Was I finally going to be sacrificed as she wanted? There were so many questions that swarmed endlessly. I knew I just had to brace myself for whatever was in store. Expect the worst. Hope for the best. This time when Eris walked forward, she no longer controlled my every movement. Instead, I chose to follow her of my own free will. There wasn't anywhere

I could've run to anyway, being that I was so far up in the sky. If I tried to flee, I could end up falling off the edge of the cliff of Mount Olympus. There were white steps that led up to the building all the way at the top. I couldn't even count them; there must've been over a thousand steps. Eris gently lifted off the ground once again and ascended the steps while I was stuck going up each one. Part of me wished she would snap her fingers and make me float again as it would have been much easier, but I was in no position to ask for any favors.

"The last thing that you said—what did you mean by saying you would fix the mess you made?" I asked on our way up.

"Is this not a mess?" she asked the obvious, avoiding the actual question I was asking.

"How do you intend on fixing it?" I made my question clearer. She slowed to a complete stop and came down to the steps again. This was the first time she had looked right into my eyes. Hers seemed to have a red glow to them.

"I am the goddess you do not hear about a lot because I seem to instigate quite a lot and break anything I touch," she said. "Your snakes… I can relate to you more than you know."

"You have snakes, too?" I stupidly asked.

"Remind me again why Percy fell for you?" she scoffed and started walking up the steps as I was. She snapped her fingers and had Percy float beside us, despite his frozen, statue-like state.

"I've been made fun of my entire life for the way I am, and I have always been a danger to everyone around me, especially the people I love most. That night at the dance, I lost my one and only friend. No one expected what happened. Especially not me."

"So you didn't unleash your snakes on everyone and turn them to stone out of hatred for humans?" she asked, stopping dead in her tracks and turning back to face me. Percy's statue continued up the steps.

"No. These boys at the dance tore my headwrap off, and that's what revealed my snakes. Just about everyone there turned to stone. I don't remember seeing you, but I ran as fast as I could. At that moment,

I wished the ground would just open up and swallow me whole." I felt a weight come off my shoulders as I vented to her. I don't think I was this honest with anyone else besides Percy. But even then, I hadn't shared that story with him.

"I have never told anyone about the love of my for fear that it would end in him getting hurt. But even so, his fate was unavoidable, I guess. Ever since that day, I had sought revenge on you in any way I could. I killed your boss at the museum not because I confused her for you, but to make sure you felt a similar pain that I had."

"And what changed now?" I asked, curious.

"No matter how much revenge I get, it won't change the fact that he's gone. I'm realizing that I actually don't want to put another soul through the heartache I had to endure that night. When I saw Percy sacrifice himself for you despite your curse, I realized that was the love I had felt for Adam all those years ago." She came closer to me and pressed her hand to my chest, directly over my heart. "You can't let a love like that go. And don't feel guilty. You were born the way that you are, and it's not your fault the others won't accept that."

"Eris." I looked at her hand and felt my heart thump, hopeful that once we reached the top of the steps, some miracle would happen. "Thank you for being the first to help me despite knowing my past."

"We're going to fix this. I promise." She winked and continued up the steps, flying just above them. She seemed to have read my mind because she snapped her fingers and I began floating above them. Just a few hours ago, I had grown to hate her with every ounce of my being, and now all I could feel for her was empathy and care. We were two sides of a coin; although very different in many ways, we shared the same foundation of a difficult past.

Once we reached the top, an enormous tower hovered over us. There were dozens of Corinthian columns that lined the outside and just a few more steps to get into the building. I began walking up before Eris. As soon as I stepped onto the gold marble floors, my reflection stared back at me.

"Hello?" My voice echoed. Behind me, I could hear Eris' footsteps as she walked on toward the statue that protruded out of the center of the room that was encased in marble. I could tell the statue was Zeus by the lightning bolt he held in one of his hands, held up high as if to strike someone down at any moment. In moments, the ground seemed to shake as if it were an earthquake. I felt relieved to see that Percy's statue was still floating above ground. If not, he would have disintegrated into pieces, and nothing would have remained of him. The statue of Zeus, however, appeared to crackle into pieces until, beneath all the pieces that fell off one by one, revealed the true Zeus.

"My daughter." He looked to Eris first. "Where is your brother, Ares?"

"Oh, you know, probably starting wars and stuff," she replied. I had just remembered that Ares and Eris were the closest brother and sister and were usually seen together. It was very rare for them to be separated. I wondered if Ares knew about her love interest that I had turned to stone.

Zeus walked over to me and peeled my headwrap off. I tried to grab it back for fear someone would get hurt, but realized I was among gods.

"No need for this here, Medusa," he chuckled. "Ah, the mortal daughter of Phorcys and Ceto."

"You knew my parents??"

"The Sea gods, yes. Consider yourself lucky you found new parents," he said.

"Well, why is that?" I couldn't help but ask.

"You are the only mortal in the family, and simply wouldn't have fit in," he replied.

"Well then, that means I don't fit in anywhere, huh?"

"Oh, shush," Eris said. "We have heard this sob story enough. Clearly you have met a family that loves you to pieces, even despite your curse."

Zeus walked over to Percy's stone statue, and I could feel the ground rumble beneath us in a rage that overthrew him when he realized just who it was.

"MY SON?!!?!?!?!" he bellowed out angrily. "What have you done?!" He immediately turned to me and put his hand around my neck, holding me in a grip hard enough to make it difficult to breathe, but not enough to kill me. I could feel my snakes struggle this way and that as they feared for my life…our lives. Zeus looked up at them, and I felt them submit almost instantly. Eris jumped in between us and held her hand to each of our chests as if trying to push us off of one another.

"Father, this is not her fault," she said.

"Then whose fault is this? I don't remember you having snakes for hair that could turn any mortal man to stone," Zeus noted the obvious.

"I turned myself in to fulfill the prophecy. To become beheaded," I revealed through stifled breaths.

"Well, you look like you've still got your head on to me. So how did that go for you? How did my *son* end up this way?" He took his hand off of my neck, walking over to Percy again. He put his head in his hands and did something I never thought I would see a grown man of his size and muscular state ever do. He wept. Aside from tears being seen as a weakness, it made him appear that much stronger. The very fact that he was able to reveal his emotions in front of others…that took some strength.

Eris went around to his side and gently put her hand on his shoulder, rubbing it in circles, comforting him. I had never seen this gentle side of her before.

"Father, it is truly all my fault. I pushed Percy to do what he didn't want to do. He had fallen in love with Meadow… Medusa. And he never intended to behead her until I gave him no choice."

"So are you saying he did this to himself? He sacrificed himself? For her?" Zeus looked back at me, eyes red and nearly bloodshot. I supposed when gods cried, it was that much more intense.

"He did. He tore her headwrap off, revealing the snakes, ultimately killing himself," Eris explained.

Just then, a wave of black smoke filled the air right behind Percy. I felt my eyes tear and couldn't stop coughing from inhaling whatever toxic fumes lay within the smoke. It billowed out into the air, and the ominous voice that I had heard back in the Underworld came out, laughing.

"I hate to be late to a party that I wasn't invited to, but can I join the fun?" he asked. When I looked at Zeus and Hades side by side, I was surprised how they could be brothers—they were strikingly different in both appearance and demeanor.

"Hades, not now," Zeus said and seemed to ponder for a moment. When he picked his head back up, he had a different expression on his face. It was no longer sadness. His face was now filled with betrayal. "How did you know they'd be here?"

"The lovebirds may have paid me a visit down in the Underworld." He looked down at his feet, declaring he was the very opposite of innocent.

"Ah, you filled my boy's head with this idea, didn't you?" Zeus crossed his arms.

"I mean, I didn't tell him what to do. He is a man of his own free will, no? Besides… Eris seems to have the blame part figured out. Let's just go with that one." He winked at Zeus and walked around to Percy's statue. "What a beautiful statue he does make, though."

I could see the anger in Zeus's eyes. And all at once, an earthquake rumbled the ground once again. I was nearly knocked over and held on to Eris' arm for balance. She didn't seem to mind as she gave me a warm, comforting look. The rumble was too much this time for Percy's statue to withstand. A small crack formed at the top of his head and traveled its way down, splitting his entire body in two. Both sides of the stone statue fell to the marbled ground and shattered into nothing at all. My grip on Eris' arm grew tighter until I had turned to her and wept into her arm. I felt her other arm wrap around me and thought back to when I was just a child, crying into my mother's arms.

"He's gone, he's really gone. I thought this could be fixed," I said, choking out each word as if Zeus still had his arm around my neck. Although this time, he no longer did, and I felt like I was choking from the emotional pain that no Band-Aid could ever help.

"Remember. Matter is neither created nor destroyed; it just goes somewhere else," she reminded me.

"But where?" I asked.

SOUL

White clouds came closer from around us until they somehow flooded into the room, causing the entire marble flooring to disappear and we were all standing in clouds. Hades stood there with an unimpressed look on his face while I moved away from Eris' embrace and my full attention was on Zeus. Both his hands were extended before him. His palms faced one another, and it was like he held an invisible ball in his hands. He moved them as if the ball were clay and he was shaping it to form the perfect circle. When I glanced over at Eris, she just nodded and looked back at Zeus. He dropped one of his hands to his side and pulled one of the thickest clouds up into his hands.

"Oh, come on, you ruin all the fun!" Hades blurted out. Zeus took a small piece of the cloud off as if it were cotton candy and sent it flying toward Hades, covering his mouth shut. Hades shook it off and scoffed, crossing his arms over his chest.

"What is he doing?" I asked, directing my question at Eris.

"You'll see." She winked at me. I couldn't take my eyes off him as he now stretched the piece of cloud he had in his hands. It stretched farther and farther until it was several feet long. He turned it so that it was a long vertical cloud column and began using his hands to shape it. It wasn't until he was shaping the head that I realized it was a person. He snapped his fingers, and the other remaining clouds pushed back out of the room, revealing the floor again. A rumbling earthquake came, except this one was different. Much, much different. I could tell it was not out of his anger and wrath, but instead, creation. Thunder came and shook the entire room, and a flash came from above. Lightning crashed down right before my eyes onto the cloud figure. The spark nearly blinded me; I had to close my eyes. Light still pierced through my closed eyes, and I wondered what was going on. I could hear my snakes hiss as they too turned away from the light.

When I reopened them, the sight that my eyes now laid upon was something I couldn't have imagined in my wildest dreams. It was something out of pure magic, but then again all of this was. I felt my mouth drop in complete shock to find who was standing before me. The man I had thought to be long gone. The man who was a stone statue and had shattered into pieces... The man that risked his life for my own.

Percy.

"My headwrap!" I screamed, frantically trying to hide behind Eris so I wouldn't cause any more problems with my snakes. She just laughed, and I heard Percy join in the laughter as if he knew, too.

"He is no longer mortal, Medusa. You do not have to hide anymore," she exclaimed.

I peeked out from behind her with just half of my body. To see that Percy was still actually there in the flesh was a sight I never thought I would see again. I walked out in the open and no longer hid, realizing he was somehow protected. Whatever Zeus had done, made him live again, but not just that, made him immortal.

"Dad?" he said, looking up at Zeus. Zeus put his arms around Percy, and I thought he'd start sobbing again, but he didn't.

"My boy," he said. "Love brings us to tricky places, doesn't it?" Percy looked over at Hades, then Eris, and seemed to realize that I was standing right next to her all along. He walked, no, ran over to me right away and enveloped me in a hug, lifting my feet up off the ground. He was much warmer to the touch than I remembered before. But everything else was just about the same. His muscular arms, dark hair... but it was those green eyes that I missed most. I pulled back and felt tears rush down my cheeks while I stared into them, not wanting to blink for a second. He just smiled back at me. Eris came up and punched him in the chest.

"That's for sacrificing yourself," she said. She punched him a second time. "And that's for scaring the daylights out of all of us."

Then, she put her arms around him and hugged him with all her might, pulling away a second later, leaving confusion in Percy's eyes.

"And lastly, that was for coming back," she noted.

"Well, it's not like I planned to come back. I just couldn't let Meadow go through with the prophecy. What is Hades doing here?" He gestured over to him just as he was sneaking out through the columns. He turned around.

"Oh, me? Well, it was a pleasure to see you in my Underworld. But stay longer next time, and you can make friends with... who was it again? Oh right. Adam. He's been there an awfully, awfully long time." He blew black smoke toward us and when it dissipated into the air, he was gone.

"I WILL GET HIM FOR THIS!" Eris shouted, blood boiling and flames dancing in her eyes. Her wings stretched out as far as they could, and she took off, gone too within seconds. I thought about the story she told me about Adam, who I had unknowingly turned to stone. That meant he was still out there. And Hades knew exactly where he was.

"What was that all about?" Percy asked.

"Eris being Eris," Zeus and I said at the same time. I could tell he already knew of her secret lover, but her secret wasn't mine to tell.

Zeus stepped toward Percy and me and laid his fist under his chin, pondering something that I couldn't even guess. Before he could say anything, I knew I had to tell him how thankful I was for what he did.

"Zeus, I will forever owe you for bringing Percy back to life. But what does this make of the prophecy?"

"The prophecy? That is broken," he said. "You have paid your debt long enough, and it is time that a new prophecy begins—the fate of you and Perseus are forever intertwined, but in a different way now," he said.

"How did you bring me back?" Percy asked.

"Boy, your soul did not want to leave this place. It just wasn't ready, but you are part of me. Being from my lineage, I can breathe life into you once more."

Zeus hugged Percy again and then took one look at me, pulling my hand toward his lips and kissing just above my knuckles. I felt a wave wash over the entirety of my being and nearly stumbled to the ground.

"If you wish to go back down to Earth, you may. You are now immortal along with Perseus. To protect others, you may camouflage as a human and turn whenever you feel you are threatened and need your power again."

I could no longer feel my snakes. Looking down into the marble that showed my reflection, they weren't there any longer. I had hair. Normal human hair. It went down to my waist. I looked at it and ran my fingers through it, realizing it was a deep, deep red shade. I tried really hard to think of the snakes again, and my red hair was no longer there. Snakes showed through my reflection. I tried to keep switching back and realized what he said was true.

I dropped to my knees as they grew weak and unable to hold me any longer. Just when I thought I had no more, tears rushed down my cheeks, and Percy kneeled beside me, holding one arm around me.

"Meadow," he said.

I looked up at him and nodded.

"You now belong not only on Earth, but here in Mount Olympus. And there is one place you will always belong." He took my hand and pressed it against his chest.

"Where?" I asked.

"Right here, in my heart. I will never leave your side again." He smiled.

That moment was when I realized just how certain I was of Percy and that love knew no bounds. Even through death, love would keep reappearing and would be everlasting. I started my life with snakes that cursed me in almost every relationship I had. Little did I know they would bring me so much fortune someday that no amount of money could ever top. Percy let out his hand and I took it, not knowing what was in store for us next, but ready to make any leap of faith with him by my side.

Love knows no bounds.

Turn the page for a sneak peek of another modern-day
retelling of a Greek Myth featuring the gods of
Death and Sleep

AVAILABLE
NOW

CHAPTER 1

TRANCE

Gentle caresses of the harp opened up the altar to a mystical place. Each note served as a guide through a forest full of life and marrow. The simple melody grasped the spectator's hearts as they, too, traveled through this forest. With each careful step, I felt closer and closer to tranquility.

A soft stroke on the black and white keys seemed to have awakened the others. The notes enveloped the once singular melody in a blanket of suppression. As the soft tone of the harp shrank, other sounds filled the air. It was all too harmonious to ignore. With careful steps,

I walked past the various people that sat in each pew, beside one another. None of them looked the same, but instead as if they came from all different paths of life. Beggars who stayed street-side left their signs to follow their ears. Their ripped clothing and drawn complexion gave their hardships away almost immediately. Doctors who must have heard the symphony from their operating rooms were sucked into a trance and found themselves in this enchanting room beside the beggars. They hadn't even stopped to take their stethoscopes or lab coats off. Couples and families that had just come from a night out at a restaurant, must have dropped their utensils the instant they heard. As the waiters saw customers leaving by the dozens, they too wandered out into the night. Soon, there would barely be enough seats for people in the cathedral-like room.

Without a word or glance, people took their seats beside one another in various pews. There was a dim light in each corner, leaving the center dark and gloomy. An altar was completely filled with orchestra members who performed without stopping. Without a conductor, they played on as if they were programmed robots repeating and repeating their notes. I watched in awe at how focused they were, but felt a bitterness in my stomach for what would soon come.

Ancient murals and stained glass windows lined the walls in the endless room. A dark statue's broad wings stretched out toward the audience. The black hooded robe that covered most of its head left me in question at what lie underneath.

On the other side of the altar was another god-like statue, but it was white in contrast. It appeared to be much more human-like if not for its wings. This statue revealed much more, as its arms were toned with muscles. It was not standing upright. Instead, it was leaning down over a person who appeared to be asleep. From my college studies of Greek mythology, I had briefly remembered Hyriad's poem of Hypnos, along with his many siblings. Hypnos was the Greek god of sleep, and the fact he stood beside someone who had been sleeping meant it was likely he had that effect on them. Without a dark cloak like the other statue had, this one had a chiton covering his body…. The entirety of his torso and waist were covered, but the smooth satin gently fell from his shoulder, revealing his muscular shoulder. The only other time I had ever seen someone with such muscles was when I would watch the Hercules cartoon as a child. A trance glazed over the orchestra and audience.

If one statue was Hypnos, it was very likely the other was Thanatos, who resembled Death.

All too suddenly, I spotted a dark shadow as it drifted across the room and wandered toward the corner. Quietly standing up from my pew, I tiptoed by the people sitting near me. *What was lurking in the corners while the others sat there, oblivious and continuously amused by the melody?*

The sudden movements I made seemed to have no effect on those around me. No one took their eyes off the stage. I could've jumped up and down while flailing my arms about in each aisle, and they still wouldn't have noticed. They didn't even blink as they watched and listened. When I reached the corner of the room where I saw the shadow, I found nothing but the dim light. I looked around at the walls and floor and saw nothing. *What happened to it?*

I drew closer toward the exit, of which I didn't even remember walking in. Towering Victorian doors stood in between my grasp of freedom. Just a few steps away and I could leave behind whatever this place was. Breathing a sigh of relief, I clung to the handle and gave it the strongest pull I could, only to find it wouldn't open. I tried pushing the handle the other way. Eventually, I dismissed the idea of having to tip-toe around and, since the others barely noticed my presence, I threw my whole body into the door, hoping it would fling open. Upon doing this a few more times, I quickly realized we were all locked in.

"Can someone help me?" I asked urgently. With no response, I looked back at the audience, still in that strange trance. No one had turned or even flinched at my voice. The orchestra continued on and now, they were violently playing at a much faster tempo.

Just then, movement danced before my eyes as I tried to follow it. I rushed to get across to the diagonal corner of the room in time. I gazed at it for only a split second before my body became weak. The shadow. I k rushed toward the other corner of the room. As soon as I reached it, it was still there. Only this time, I stood next to it for a split second and in the next, I could barely feel anything as my body went completely numb. At first, my legs felt like bags of sand as I tried to lift them to move. Gradually, the entirety of my being felt as though I was no longer in control. When I looked down at my feet, they were turning dark and lifeless. A shadow seemed to extend up from there, taking away any remaining sign of life from me. When the darkness spread up to my waist, I yelped, surprised my mouth could still move. No one answered as they stayed entranced in the melody that was still ongoing.

Before I knew it, my entire body was wrapped in the shadow. What felt even worse than no longer being in control of my body was the fact there was no one that would save me. Although the room was full to capacity, not one soul broke out of the music's grasp to come save me. No one could hear me. No one could help. I tried pushing myself to run away or find another way to escape, but it was too late. I was merely a shadow in the room. A lifeless shadow no one could see.

Though my eyes were wide open, I couldn't seem to blink. In the very corner of my eye, something was missing. Despite the people staying in their pews, the statues that towered over them were no longer there. Without being able to move, I was forced to look frantically around in the same spot over and over again. I hoped I was only seeing things or someone was playing a trick on me. The statues had been there...hadn't they? I remember walking by them and there wasn't the slightest bit of movement from either. As the music mirrored my heart in its racing beat, footsteps that I had almost mistaken for drums—although there were none on the altar—approached. When I looked back at the audience, they were no longer staring at the altar...but instead, their eyes were glued to me. A woman that sat beside her child in one of the front pews had glossy eyes, as if she somehow could still convey emotion despite being paralyzed. It appeared as though she was trying to fight whatever was causing the paralysis that immobilized her, along with everyone else in the room...even me. The footsteps I had once heard ceased along with the music and the entire room was no longer focused on the orchestra that had been playing continuously through all of this. Dark wings extended into my view; swiftly folding back as the hooded man crept before me. Somehow, the statue was no longer frozen in position as it had been. It was moving. It was real. I wasn't able to see his face since his hood remained over his head as he looked down at the ground. The coldness of his body matched his previously frozen state, but his movements were similar to that of a soldier…unbending and marching closer to me. He reached out his hand as if expecting me to take it willingly. Although I still couldn't feel my body, I saw my arm raise in the corner of my eye. I was no longer in control of what I was doing. He controlled me while I placed my hand atop his cold, pale fingers. With his other hand, he took mine and turned me around. I could no longer see what he was doing, and it raged me to no end. In the next second, I was no longer standing but instead, looking at the ground from over his shoulder. He had effortlessly draped me over his arm as if I were nothing other than a towel. I wanted to kick and scream…tear my nails into him…and break free. But I couldn't. As he continued to walk in front of the audience, I locked eyes with a man that held a violin under his chin. He seemed to be in a frozen state, too. But this man differed from the rest because I felt like I had seen him before. He was staring straight back at me with worry in his eyes, just as the woman had. Before I could gaze at him any longer, the dark-winged man turned and walked a few more steps before he reached a pew where he plumped me down on. Although I wasn't able to move my positioning, his cold hands grasped mine as he placed them on my lap and gently touched my chin to move it up, as if to watch the performance along with everyone else. While I had expected violence from this man, his fingertips felt more sensitive to the touch than anything I had felt before. The audience still looked as though they were in a trance before me, but their bodies were also dark and lifeless. We were all just shadows in the room; lost and forgotten.

As the dark-winged statue left, the other one with white wings, in contrast, peered out from the side of the pew. He looked expressionless, just as the other had. His movements were much slower and deliberate. He seemed different from the other statue in that he locked eyes with me while the other had avoided any eye contact. When he walked toward me, he pressed his cold hand to my forehead. Right before he seemed to have any effect on me, I could feel one salty tear trail down my cheek and onto my lips. I felt tranquility envelop me into a state of dormancy. It was then that I realized I was now cemented to this pew, along with everyone else in the room.

ACKNOWLEDGEMENTS

Thank you to those that I have lost for always sending reminders even when you are no longer here physically. I couldn't have done this without you.

I am grateful for the Maryland Writing Association for providing countless workshops and networking opportunities to learn more about publishing and writing.

Thank you to my family and friends for supporting me on my writing journey and always cheering me on. I couldn't do it without you!